DONOVAN'S WOMAN

AMANDA ASHLEY

Donovan's Woman
Copyright © 2016 Amanda Ashley
All rights reserved.

Published by Butterfly Kisses Press
Cover design by Matt Forsyth
ISBN: 1680680048
ISBN-13: 978-1680680041

CHAPTER 1

The woman with the long golden-blonde hair was still sitting at the end of the bar when the last sky pilot staggered out of the place. Gryff Donovan shook his head. He didn't know who in blazes she was, but as sure as white tigers ran wild in the jungles of Brynn Tor, she didn't belong in a two-bit dive like this. She was too quiet, too polite, and looked far too innocent. So, who in hell was she? And what in blue blazes was she doing in a slag heap like Ironntown?

Picking up a rag, Gryff began to wipe the bar top, hoping she would take the hint and get lost so he could close up. But she just continued to sit there, staring into her empty glass as if it held the answers to all the mysteries in the galaxy.

Damn and blast. He was going to have to throw her out.

Tossing the rag aside, he moved toward the end of the bar.

The woman didn't stir, didn't look up at his approach.

"We're closing," he said curtly. "That'll be three credits for the drink."

Lifting her head, she met his gaze.

Gryff swore softly. She had the most beautiful eyes he had ever seen. Large and almond-shaped, they were a brilliant blue-green, as clear as the Brynn Sea at sunrise. Sad eyes bright with unshed tears.

Damn and blast! The last thing he needed was to get involved with some lost soul.

Leaning forward, he crossed his arms on the scuffed bar top. "You want to talk about it?" Listening came with the territory. He had lost track of the number of sob stories he had heard in the last five months.

She stared at him blankly. "Excuse me?"

"Something's troubling you. You want to talk about it before you go?"

"Go?" A single tear slipped down one pale cheek. "Where should I go?"

Gryff dragged a hand across his beard-roughened jaw. He hadn't shaved in a couple of days, but what did it matter? "Home?" he suggested.

"I…" A second tear followed the first, promising a flood to come. "I don't know where that is."

"You lost?"

"I guess I must be."

He blew out a sigh. "You got a name?"

"Of course. Everyone has a name…" She hunched her shoulders as a sob racked her slender frame. "I just can't remember what mine is."

Damn and double damn. If he were smart, he'd throw her out on her curvy little butt and lock the door behind her. Too bad he had never been smart where pretty women were concerned. If he had been, he wouldn't be holed up here now, in the arm pit of the galaxy, serving drinks to sky pirates and marauders.

"Listen, it's closing time," he said. "So…?"

"Oh, of course. I'm so sorry." She stared up at him. "I can't pay…"

"Forget it."

He followed her out the front door, locked it behind him. He hadn't gone ten steps when something made him glance over his shoulder. She stood where he'd left her, gazing off into the distance.

Shit! No money. No place to stay. He couldn't just leave her standing in front of the bar, prey to pirates and wild animals.

Backtracking, he placed his hand on her shoulder. "Come on," he said, "you can spend the night at my place."

"That's very kind of you, but I couldn't."

"Suit yourself."

She stared up at him, eyes wide and uncertain.

"You might want to reconsider. I know we've just met, but, unlike some of the creatures that come after dark, I promise not to eat you."

"Thank you for your offer of hospitality," she said.

Nodding, he headed for the winding gravel path that led to the rundown shack he currently called home. It wasn't much to look at, inside or out, but he could come and go as he pleased and that was a big plus.

Inside, he switched on the room's single light, heard the familiar skittering as the roaches that shared the house with him scurried into the shadows.

He didn't miss the look of revulsion on the woman's face as she glanced at her surroundings. He didn't know who she was, but he would have bet his last credit that she had never been in a dump like this in her life. And it was a dump, from the uneven dirt floor to the drooping ceiling. The amenities were scarce - a faded green divan, a rough-hewn, three-legged wooden table, and a chair. A single barred window looked out on the barren desert. A small stove and a solar refrigerator stood in one corner.

Well, he'd seen better places in his time, too. But he much preferred freedom in a roach-infested shack to the life he had known before, where every day had been a fight to survive. Hell, he had the scars to prove it.

He jerked a thumb toward the curtain that divided his living quarters from the bedroom. "You can have the bed."

"Thank you." She stared at him a moment, as if trying to decide if she knew him or not, then stepped behind the ragged brown curtain.

She was a strange one, he mused as he shrugged out of his jacket and tossed it over the back of the room's only chair. Sitting down on the lumpy divan, he pulled off his boots and reached for a cigarette. He lit it, took a deep drag, and sighed with pleasure. With the price of imported cigarettes, he couldn't afford more than one smoke a day. It was his one vice, and his one indulgence.

He took another drag, his mind wandering to the woman. She seemed disoriented, maybe a little muddled. Well, it didn't matter. She could spend the night here and then she was on her own. He had enough to worry about, what with Serepta's informers and guards scouring the western territory looking for him, though it seemed unlikely that anyone would look for him in this godforsaken place. Still, it paid to be cautious because he sure as hell wasn't going back to being Serepta's lap dog!

He smoked the cigarette down until it burned his fingers, stubbed it out on the dirt floor, and stretched out on the lumpy couch, his thoughts turning toward the distant, snow-covered mountains of home. Some day, he thought as he drifted off to sleep, some day he would see them again.

She sat on the edge of the bed, her head cradled in her hands. What had made her agree to stay with this man? And yet, unless she wanted to sleep outside, what other choice did she have? And why, oh why, couldn't she remember who she was?

Sometimes she could almost remember her name, but as soon as she tried to grasp it, it slipped through her fingers like smoke in the wind.

Why couldn't she remember?

She ran her hand over the poorly woven material of her long brown skirt. It felt alien to her touch, as if some part of her knew that she was used to finer things. Had she truly chosen such a dreadful frock? And in such a dismal hue? But then, for all she knew, muddy brown might be her favorite color.

She glanced at her surroundings. How could anyone live like this? There were reddish-brown stains on the walls; she didn't even want to think what might have left marks like that. The floor was dirt. No spread covered the bed, just a moth-eaten, gray wool blanket. No drapery at the single, narrow window, and only the stub of a candle for light. The three-drawer chest was missing one drawer.

Tears stung her eyes. She told herself it was useless to cry. It would solve nothing, change nothing, but still the tears came, rolling down her cheeks faster and faster, until she was sobbing uncontrollably. She was lost on a barren planet. She didn't know who she was. And she was sitting in a room that was barely fit for human habitation.

"Here now, what's wrong?"

She looked up, startled to see her benefactor staring down at her. He had a nice voice, she thought absently, in spite of its gruff tone. It resonated deep within her.

She tensed as he sat on the bed beside her. Stars above, was he expecting some intimacy from her in exchange for a place to spend the night?

"Take it easy," he said in that same gruff tone. "I'm not gonna hurt you." Pulling the black kerchief from around his neck, he wiped the tears from her cheeks. "What's wrong, honey?"

She stared at him, startled by the unexpected endearment. What was wrong? She didn't know who she was or where she was, couldn't remember how she had come to be in his establishment, or what had possessed her to agree to stay in his house. What was wrong, she thought, teetering on the edge of hysteria. What wasn't?

Muttering an oath, he drew her into his arms and patted her back as if she were a child.

For a moment, she remained rigid, then slowly relaxed against him. There was nothing threatening in his touch. His hand, though callused and twice the size of hers, was gentle as it slid up and down her back. He smelled of tobacco and sweat. She was sure there had been a time when she would have found his odor distasteful but it was oddly comforting now, as was the steady beating of his heart and the feel of his broad chest beneath her cheek.

"I'm guessing you've got some form of amnesia," he remarked after a time. "Either that or someone drugged you to make you forget who you are. Either way, your memory will probably come back in a few days."

She didn't know whether to believe him or not. He could be lying. For all she knew, he could have been the one who drugged her. Still, his words made her feel a little better.

"How about if I call you Cay?" he asked.

She repeated the name in her mind. *Cay.* It was pretty, but totally unfamiliar. She sniffed, then nodded her approval. "And what should I call you?"

"Gryff."

"I'm pleased to meet you, Mr. Gryff." He was a handsome man, with his long blue-black hair and tawny skin. A thin white scar bisected his left cheek. A second scar ran down the right side of his neck and disappeared beneath his shirt. Strangely, instead of marring his appearance, the slight disfigurements added a touch of rugged masculinity she found oddly appealing. It was hard to judge his age, but she guessed he was in his mid-thirties.

"Just Gryff," he said.

He smiled at her and something warm and totally unfamiliar blossomed deep within her, making her feel as if she had swallowed a piece of the sun.

"Why don't you try and get some sleep?" he said, rising.

She nodded. "Thank you for everything."

"Sure, kid."

She stared up at him, thinking there was something strange about his eyes. Earlier, in the tavern, she would have sworn they were dark brown but now they looked almost gold. She shook her head. It was bad enough she didn't know who she was. Now she was imagining things.

He brushed a wisp of hair from her cheek, then glanced out the window. She followed his gaze, though she could see nothing through the dirty glass but the faint silvery light of the moon peeking through the clouds. She felt him tense a moment and then, without another word, he turned on his heel and left the room.

She stared after him, puzzled by his abrupt departure. With a sigh, she stood and went to the window. What had he seen out there? She glanced left and right, but saw only the rising moon playing hide and seek with the drifting clouds. Here and there, a few stars were visible.

She was about to go back to bed when a movement from outside drew her attention. Leaning forward, she saw a large black wolf standing only a few feet away from the shack. It stared at her through golden eyes for a long moment, then turned and trotted away, disappearing into the scrub brush beyond.

Jerking back from the window, she hurried back to bed and pulled the covers up to her chin. A moment later, a wolf's mournful howl lifted the fine hairs along her nape.

Chapter 2

The wolf paused in the shadows, nostrils testing the air, hackles rising when he spied two men clad in dark clothing skulking toward the shack. He watched as they deftly picked the lock, paused a moment, then opened the door.

A low growl rose in the wolf's throat when the two intruders stepped inside. Belly to the ground, he moved toward the shack, pausing briefly inside the doorway, ears twitching. He could hear muted voices as the two men moved deeper into the building's gloomy interior.

A muffled cry drew the wolf into the bedroom. The woman thrashed about on the bed, arms flailing in an effort to fend off the burly man who was holding her down. Apparently tiring of her struggles, the man struck her, knocking her unconscious. With a grunt, the second man drew a wicked-looking knife from the inside of his boot.

The wolf didn't need to see any more. He launched himself at the man wielding the knife, his fangs sinking deep into the assassin's throat, ripping out his jugular. Blood fountained from the killing wound, spraying the floor, the walls, and the wolf.

The second man whirled around and ran for his life, but he wasn't fast enough. Before he reached the door, the wolf was on him, jaws closing around the man's nape. A quick twist broke the assassin's neck.

The smell of blood and urine fouled the air.

Sitting back on his haunches, the wolf let out a long, low howl. Then, tail wagging, he went back into the bedroom and sniffed the woman. She was still unconscious but seemed unhurt, save for a few bruises on her arms and face.

With a low growl, the wolf returned to the main room. Seizing the dead man's shoulder in his jaws, he dragged the corpse out of the shack and into the desert beyond.

When the wolf returned for the second man, the woman was sitting up on the bed, one hand pressed to her swollen jaw.

Cay's eyes widened when the black wolf padded into the bedroom. She glanced around, seeking another exit, felt a shock of recognition when she looked at the dead man sprawled on the floor. As if blinders had been stripped from her eyes and her mind, she knew who the dead man was and, more importantly, who she was. Her name wasn't Cay, it was Marri of House Treymanne. Her father, Leonid, was king of Brynn Tor. Had Gryff recognized her? Was that why he had brought her here? Was there a reward for her return? Judging from her surroundings, the barkeep could certainly use a few extra credits.

But there was no point in worrying about Gryff, not now, not when the biggest wolf she had ever seen was standing no more than an arm's length away, its head canted to one side as it regarded her through unblinking yellow-gold eyes.

Heart pounding with fear, she stared at the creature, wondering if it was the same beast she had seen through the window earlier. As far back as she could remember, she had been afraid of wolves, though she couldn't remember why. Her father had told her she had nothing to fear from the wolves that roamed the hills and mountains at home. He had assured her time and again that the animals didn't attack people. If she ever saw her father again, she would tell him that he had been mistaken.

She glanced at the dead man again. His throat had been ripped out. Judging from the wolf's bloody muzzle and the blood smeared on its chest, she had little doubt the wolf had killed Trist. What had happened to the second man? Had the creature killed him? Would it kill her, too?

Her gaze darted around the room a second time, anxiously seeking a weapon, but there was nothing save the bed she occupied and the stub of a candle on the crude bedside table.

Feeling completely helpless and vulnerable, she drew the covers up to her chin, and waited.

The wolf looked at her, its tongue lolling out of the side of its mouth in a wolfish grin. And then it took hold of the dead man's leg and dragged the body out of the room.

For a moment, Marri fell back on the pillow, weak with relief, and then she scrambled to her feet. She had to get out of here, now, before the wolf came back, before more of Artur's men found her.

Her hand flew to her mouth as she realized that she hadn't seen or heard Gryff. Had the wolf killed him, too?

Afraid of what she might find, she hurried into the other room. The door was ajar. There was no sign of the second assassin or the black wolf. And no sign of Gryff.

The open door left her feeling exposed. She was about to cross the room and close it when Gryff appeared in the doorway.

Startled by his abrupt appearance, she took a quick step backward.

"Sorry," he muttered. "Didn't mean to scare you."

She stared at the blood on his hands and at the crimson smear across the bottom of his right cheek. "Are you all right?"

"Sure, why?"

"You're bleeding."

"It's not mine," he said flatly.

She didn't know what to make of that.

After wiping his hands on his trousers, he grabbed a towel and mopped the blood from his face. "Go on back to bed."

"I can't stay here."

He kicked the door shut with his heel. "Why not?"

"I just can't." She knew who she was now, knew why those men had tried to kill her. When Artur's assassins didn't return, he would send someone else, and he would keep sending his men after her until she was dead.

She had to leave now, had to make her way to Tarnn. She would be safe there, with Annis, until she could figure out who, if anyone, she could trust at home.

She met Gryff's gaze. "Thank you for everything, but I must go."

He looked at her, his eyes narrowed. "Those men are dead."

How did he know about Trist and the other man? Was the wolf a pet?

Before she could question him, he closed the distance between them. Her heart skipped a beat when his fingertips lightly stroked her swollen jaw.

"They can't hurt you any more."

His touch sent an unexpected rush of longing through her, a sudden yearning to be held, to know that she wasn't alone. Her gaze darted to his mouth. What would it be like if he kissed her? What would he think if she kissed him?

Shocked by her wayward thoughts, she backed away from him. "What do you know about those men?" Was Gryff in league with Artur? Was that how he had known about Trist? No doubt Dakkar had been the second assassin. They often hunted together.

Too agitated to remain still, she began to pace the floor. Was there no one she could trust?

"It doesn't matter what I know," Gryff said quietly. "You're safe now."

She shook her head. "No." Feeling suddenly chilled, she scrubbed her hands up and down her arms.

He regarded her speculatively for several moments. "Is there something you're not telling me?"

"No," she said, wide-eyed. "Of course not."

"Why don't I believe you?"

"Are you calling me a liar?" she asked, her voice thick with righteous indignation.

"Sounds that way."

She stared at him, speechless. In all her life, no one had ever talked to her like that. Had she been at home, she would have had him flogged. But she wasn't home, she was…where? Even with her memory restored, she had no idea where she was or how to find her way to Tarnn. But it didn't matter. She couldn't stay here.

"You okay, princess?"

"Why did you call me that?" she asked sharply, then blew out a breath. She was over-reacting. There was no way he could know who she was.

He frowned at her, then shrugged.

"Well, thanks again," she said. "I'm going now."

Gryff made a sweeping gesture toward the door. "Don't let it hit you on the butt on the way out."

With a nod that could only be called regal, she opened the door and stepped out of the shack.

Gryff stared after her. He should feel relieved, he thought. And he was. Relieved that those two killers had been after her and not him.

Kicking the door closed, he reached for a cigarette and lit it. He took a long, deep drag. Damn and blast, what was he thinking, to let her go off alone like that? He still didn't know who she was, though he wouldn't be surprised to learn she was royalty. She had that air about her.

Damn! What was he doing, standing here smoking a cigarette, when someone obviously wanted her dead?

He told himself he didn't care. It had nothing to do with him. But he couldn't forget the frightened look in those blue-green eyes, or the way she had felt in his arms.

Knowing he was probably going to regret it, he tossed his cigarette into the fireplace, grabbed his jacket, and went after the woman.

Marri walked away from the tavern, stopping only when it was out of sight. She felt a sense of hopelessness as she glanced around. She had no idea where she was, or which way to go, or where she could find help that she could trust.

She didn't know anything about finding her way in a strange place. Never before, in all her three and twenty years, had she ever been away from the safety of her home, never associated with anyone who wasn't a trusted friend or a member of her family. Maybe she should go back to Gryff. In spite of the recent attack by Artur's assassins, she had felt safe with him. Even though he was obviously of peasant stock, she was sure he would protect her with his life, if necessary. Or was she just imagining things? After all, what did she really know about the man? Or about men, for that matter?

She was still trying to decide what course to take when she had the unshakeable feeling that she was no longer alone.

Fear came quickly - a sudden churning in the pit of her stomach, a coldness in her limbs.

Someone was behind her. She was sure of it! Were there more of Artur's men out there, watching her?

Reason vanished, replaced by surging panic and the innate instinct for survival. With a wordless cry, she bolted into the darkness, her only thought to escape whatever stalked her in the night.

She screamed as a heavy hand closed over her arm.

"Hush, it's me."

She relaxed instantly at the sound of his voice. Anger quickly replaced relief.

"What do you mean, creeping up on me like that?"

"Hey, I'm sorry, princess."

"What were you thinking, to scare me so?"

"I'm thinking I should have left you out here alone, that's what I'm thinking," he retorted.

That was the last thing she wanted. "No, please…"

"Where are you headed?"

"To Tarnn."

"Tarnn?" he exclaimed. "That's way the hell and gone on the other side of the Brynn Sea. How the hell did you get here?"

"I don't know." She lifted a hand to her head. "It's all so vague."

"What's the last thing you remember?"

She frowned. "I was getting ready for bed. Talitha brought me a cup of tea…I don't remember anything after that until I found myself in your establishment."

He grunted softly. "Who's Talitha?"

"She was my nanny when I was a child. Now's she my chambermaid."

"Sounds like she drugged you."

"Don't be absurd. Talitha has been in our family for years. Why, she was born in the keep only a few years before I was."

The keep. Gryff swore softly. Damn and blast, maybe she really was a princess!

"You don't really think she would…" Marri broke off, unable to say the words. It was beyond reason that Talitha would do such a despicable thing, and yet…who else could have done it? Talitha always tasted everything before offering it to Marri…no! It couldn't be true. She wouldn't believe it, couldn't believe it. If she couldn't trust Talitha, then she couldn't trust anyone.

"We can't stand out here all night," Gryff said. "Come on back to my place. We'll leave in the morning."

"You'll take me to Tarnn?"

He nodded. Hell, if she really was a princess, there was likely a nice reward involved, and he could sure as hell use it.

Marri stared at him. She didn't want to go back to that horrible shack. Men had died there, men who had been sent to kill her, but it seemed wiser than tromping off through the desert in the dead of night by herself. She didn't know where that wolf was, or what other dangerous creatures might be lurking in the shadows, ready to pounce on her. Murmuring her thanks to Gryff, she lifted her skirts and followed him back to the shack.

Later, lying alone in the dark, she wondered if she had made the right decision. What did she know about Gryff, really? Nothing, she thought, nothing at all. Except for the shivery way he made her feel. It occurred to her that, in his way, Gryff might prove even more dangerous than Artur's assassins.

Chapter 3

Marri woke at first light to find Gryff standing beside the bed. She stared up at him, wondering what he was doing in her bedroom, and then she remembered - he wasn't in her bedroom. She was in his.

She drew the covers up to her chin, trying not to notice the width of his shoulders beneath his long-sleeved black shirt, or the way his faded trousers hugged his long legs. She clenched her hands, stifling the unexpected urge to reach out and run her fingers over his beard-roughened jaw, down his long, muscular arms.

"Get up," he said without preamble. "We're leaving."

With a nod, she pushed the covers aside and reached for her shoes. Last night, feeling troubled and uneasy in her mind, she had slept fully clothed.

Rising, she tried to smooth the wrinkles from her skirt even though she knew it was useless. Never in her life had she felt so dirty and disheveled. Did he think she always looked this way, Marri wondered, and then chastised herself for caring. His opinion of her was of no consequence.

Wordlessly, he thrust a thick slice of dry brown bread into her hand.

She stared at it with distaste, her mouth watering when she recalled the enormous breakfasts Malia had prepared ~ poached eggs, wafer-thin slices of ham, honey cakes and peppermint tea.

When her stomach growled, Marri took a bite, thinking wistfully of fluffy scones, warm from the oven and smothered in butter and wild honey.

Marri sighed. No point in hoping for what she couldn't have. At the moment, she was lucky to have a piece of bread. She was surprised to find it tasted better than it looked. At any rate, she was too anxious to be on her way to worry about breakfast. The sooner they left this place, the sooner she would reach Tarnn and the safety of Aisley Cloister, where her older sister, had taken her vows.

Marri followed Gryff into the other room. He swung a pack over his shoulder, glanced back to make sure she was behind him, and left the shack.

Outside, Marri blinked against the early morning light. Overhead, the sky was a bold, bright blue. Rolling foothills loomed in the distance, barren and brown beneath the harsh desert sun. A few spindly trees near the shack provided scant shade.

Marri shook her head. Why would anyone want to live in this desolate place?

"Let's go."

She looked at Gryff, standing beside a two-man Landskiff. Surely he didn't intend for them to travel in *that* old thing? It was rusty and dented; the windshield was cracked, one of the front lights hunk askew.

He shrugged as if reading her mind. "It's this or your own two feet," he remarked sardonically. "And it's a hell of a long walk to Tarnn."

She waited for him to open the door for her. When he didn't, she reached a tentative hand toward the handle, half-expecting it to fall off in her grasp, surprised when it didn't.

Gryff climbed in the other side, tossed his pack behind the seat, and fired the engine. The whole craft shook as it coughed and sputtered to life. He had to admit, it wasn't much of a vehicle, but it had been the best thing he could steal on such short notice. It would have been faster to hop a transport to Tarnn but that required tickets and identification. He didn't know about Marri, but he didn't have any papers and he didn't dare show his face in a space port, not with Serepta's bloodhounds on the prowl. The last time he had considered using a transport, he had seen his photo and description posted at the ticket window.

Marri grabbed hold of the door handle, hanging on for dear life as the craft shot forward. Walking might have taken longer, she thought, but it would undoubtedly have been much safer.

Gryff turned to her after an extended silence. "So, why don't you tell me about yourself? How'd you wind up here, in the armpit of the galaxy?"

"I told you, I don't remember."

He grunted softly. "Any idea who sent those guys after you?"

Shrugging, she glanced out the grimy window. Should she tell him the truth? Did she dare trust him? She didn't know a single thing about him. What would he do if he knew her younger brother was trying to usurp the throne? Though she had no proof, she was certain that Artur had killed their two older brothers. Caddin had gone hunting one morning and never returned. She could still remember her horror when his body had been brought home. The physician said he'd broken his neck, likely in a fall from his horse. Marri had refused to believe that was the cause of death. Caddin had been an excellent horseman. There was no horse he couldn't ride. He had never been thrown.

She had been equally horrified when her other brother, Cobb, had been found dead in his mistress's bed a little more than a month later, the same day Orlani had mysteriously disappeared. Artur had claimed that was proof of Orlani's guilt, but again, Marri refused to believe it. Orlani might have been Cobb's mistress, but Marri knew her brother and Orlani had been very much in love, though they could never wed.

When Marri's mother, Amerris, learned of the death of her second son, she had gone into deep mourning and left the keep. Cobb had always been her favorite child. No one, not even Marri's father, knew where Amerris had gone.

Marri had voiced her suspicions about Artur to her father, but he had refused to listen to anything she said. Artur was a quiet, gentle boy, her father had insisted vehemently. Everyone from the lowliest housemaid to the parish priest knew Artur was harmless. Why, he wasn't even strong enough to participate in battle games with the other men. The mere sight of blood sickened him so that he stayed behind when the knights went hunting or rode off to war.

But Marri had seen the other side of her youngest brother, the side that tortured helpless animals and bullied the servants when no one else was looking. He delighted in frightening the keep's children.

She frowned, wondering why Artur hadn't killed her outright, as he had Caddin and Cobb. She blinked back tears. In spite of what she knew of Artur, in spite of what she suspected, she still found it hard to believe that he had killed her brothers and wanted her dead, as well. He was the baby of the family, born four years after Marri. He had been such a sweet infant, such an adorable little boy with his tawny hair and bright blue eyes. She had loved him with all her heart. How could he have turned into such a monster? And how could she convince her father that the lad he doted on was a murderer?

She shook her head. Surely she was mistaken. Despite everything, she couldn't make herself believe her brother meant to kill her. She had no designs on the throne, wanted only to join her sister at the cloister. Indeed, she would have done so years ago if her father hadn't objected. He had given one daughter to the church, he had said adamantly, and that was enough.

"You're gonna have to tell me what's going on if you want my help," Gryff said, breaking into her troubled thoughts. "I have to know what we're up against, who else might be after you, and why."

She hesitated a moment before answering. "I think it's my little brother, Artur."

Gryff looked at her, one brow arched. "Your brother? What'd you ever do to him?"

"Nothing. He's…he's unstable. You know, not quite right in his head." It wasn't a lie, not entirely. She had once seen her brother throw a kitten from one of the tower windows just to see if the animal would land on its feet. It might have been excused as a youthful prank had Artur not been a man fully grown at the time.

She felt Gryff watching her, waiting for her to go on.

Marri folded her arms over her chest. She couldn't tell him the truth, couldn't tell him that Artur's lust for the throne had turned him into a killer. Not until she knew him better. Not until she knew, without a doubt, that Artur had hired those two assassins.

"It's the truth!" she exclaimed, discomfited by his unblinking gaze.

"Lady, I can smell a lie a mile away, and that one stinks."

She felt a rush of heat climb into her cheeks. "That's the second time you've called me a liar!"

He shrugged. "I call 'em as I see 'em."

"He wants to kill me," she said, "but only because he's troubled in his mind."

"Okay, princess, if that's the way you want it."

She looked at him sharply, wondering again if he knew who she was. But how could he? He couldn't. It was impossible. With a sigh, she looked out the window again, her thoughts as dreary as the countryside.

Gryff concentrated on the road, which had become increasingly rough. He couldn't force her to tell him anything, he thought, then grunted softly. No doubt he could force her, but the idea didn't appeal to him. One thing he knew for sure, she was afraid of more than a younger brother who wasn't quite right in the head.

He slowed the Landskiff. The road was little more than dirt and rocks at this point. The trees that grew in the area were stunted and dry. There was no other vegetation to speak of save for a few dried husks and shriveled plants.

He hated this place. Perhaps, after he'd seen the woman safely to Tarnn, he would go home. He could see it clearly in his mind, the tall mountains, the rivers that ran blue and clear both summer and winter, the trees that were ever green, the multitude of flowers that dotted the hillsides, the lacy ferns that grew along the lakes and streams. It was a verdant land, green all year long except in the high mountains where it snowed during the winter.

"What are you thinking about?" Marri asked.

"Home." He answered without thinking.

"I thought the tavern was…?"

"Hell, no."

"Have you been away a long time?"

"More than five years."

"Where do you live?"

"In the mountains of Nardinnia." Once, his family had raised the best cattle and the most coveted horses on the planet. But Serepta had put an end to that.

"Do you have people there?" Marri asked. He seemed like such a solitary man, she couldn't picture him as part of a family.

He shook his head. They were all gone now, destroyed by Serepta in a fit of pique.

"Why don't you go back?"

"I can't." It was the first place Serepta would look for him.

Serepta. She was a witch without equal. Thinking of her, of what she had put him through, sent a shudder of revulsion down his spine.

She had told him once that, should he ever escape, she would not rest until she found him again.

"And I will find you," she had said, her voice as cold as Brynn Tor's icy sea. "I will find you and flay the flesh from your bones an inch at a time. And then I will heal you and do it again."

One look into her hell-black eyes and he had known she meant every word. But it hadn't kept him from trying to escape at every opportunity, no matter the risk. She had chastised him each time, each punishment worse than the last, but he had craved his freedom the way some men craved drugs, had been willing to endure any pain, any torture she could devise, to be rid of her. She had burned his flesh with hot irons. She had whipped him until his back was raw. She had kept him chained in a small, dark room until he thought he would go mad. It had been the worst torture of all.

Lost in thought, Gryff paid little heed to the woman until he heard her stomach growling.

He slid a glance in her direction. "We'll stop at the next tavern and get something to eat."

She murmured a quiet thank you, then went back to looking out the window.

Gryff blew out a sigh, wondering what in blazes had prompted him to offer to take her to Tarnn in the first place. Though he had no love for tending bar in a rundown tavern, he had been relatively safe there, responsible for no one but himself.

He glanced at Marri once again. Her hair fell down her back in a thick braid, her skin golden brown and unblemished, her features delicate but not weak, and her figure…it was nicely rounded in all the right places.

He shook his head. Women! The ones he had known in the past had been nothing but trouble.

He had a feeling deep in his gut that this one would be no different.

CHAPTER 4

Artur paced the floor of the great hall, his agitation growing with every step. Dakkar and Trist should have returned from Ironntown with news of his sister death by now. The fact that they were late could only mean one of two things: either they had been unable to find Marri and were afraid to return and face his wrath, or they were dead.

Going to the door, Artur summoned his bodyguard. Dunnin was a big brute of a man, with white hair, cold gray eyes, massive arms, and legs like tree trunks. Artur shook his head as he regarded the man. For all his size, Dunnin was amazingly quick in both mind and body.

The bodyguard bowed when he entered the room. "How may I be of service, my lord?"

"You're the only man I dare trust with his," Artur said. He was, in fact, the only man in the keep that he trusted at all. "Dakkar and Trist should have returned by now. Their last transmission was day before yesterday. Take as many men as you need and go to Ironntown. If Dakkar and Trist are dead, I want to know who killed them. If they're alive, find out where my sister is, and then kill them all. Don't fail me."

With a bow, Dunnin backed out of the room and closed the door.

Artur went to the window and stared into the distance. He should have killed Marri when he had the chance. Instead, he'd had her drugged, then ordered two of his most trusted men to dispose of her in any way they saw fit as long as her body could not be recovered. His gut told him they had failed and now Marri was out there somewhere.

"Ah, Marri. Marri," he murmured, as he paced the floor. "As much as it grieves me, I cannot allow you to return to the keep." For all that she was only a woman, he mused, she was no fool. He knew she suspected he had killed both Caddin and Cobb, though she could never prove it. He had been far too clever for that. "I dare not take any chances, sister, not now, when I am so close." It was a difficult decision, but one rulers were expected to make. In order for him to take the throne, she had to be eliminated before she could voice her suspicions again.

He gave no thought to his father. The King was old and sickly. News of Marri's demise would undoubtedly send the old fool to his deathbed. His mother was no threat. Even if anyone knew of her whereabouts, she could never attain the throne. The line of power passed from father to child.

Smiling at his reflection in the window pane, Artur adjusted his cloak, flicked a bit of lint from his shirtfront. There was nothing to worry about. Dunnin had never failed him.

Soon his sister would no longer be a threat. It saddened him that she had to die. She had ever been kind to him but, like all women, she was unimportant in the grand scheme of things.

Turning, he glanced around the great hall. This was the seat of power. It was in this room that his father issued formal decrees, pardoned or condemned those accused of crimes, welcomed foreign emissaries, accepted gifts from his subjects.

Artur's gaze rested on the many tapestries that hung from the walls, each one depicting scenes of victory from the battles of the former kings of Brynn Tor. Large stone hearths stood at each end of the hall. Carpets and rushes covered the floor, the windows were of stained glass imported from Brazia. Long trestle tables lined the walls. A longbow that had belonged to the first ruler of Brynn Tor hung over the fireplace on the eastern wall. It was the ancient symbol of authority and as such, had been passed from one ruler to the next.

His gaze continued around the room, coming to rest on his

father's throne. It stood on a raised dais at the southern end of the room. It was a remarkable piece of craftsmanship, carved from a single tree and inscribed with the name of every man who had ever worn the crown. The seat and back were covered in rich dark purple, the color of royalty.

Filled with a sense of pride and power, he stepped onto the dais and sat on the throne, his hands resting on the carved arms. Soon, the kingdom would be his, the throne would be his, with no one left to challenge his power, his authority, or his right to rule as he saw fit.

He would allow no one, not even his beloved sister, to keep him from the throne.

CHAPTER 5

Gryff parked the Landskiff on the side of the road, stepped out, and stretched his back and shoulders. Rounding the front of the craft, he looked in the cockpit window and saw Marri staring back at him. "You all right in there?"

She nodded.

He looked at her a moment, then grunted softly as he realized that she expected him to open the door for her. He did so with a grimace.

"Don't get used to it," he muttered irritably, and with a shake of his head, he turned his back on her and sauntered into the tavern.

Gryff glanced at his surroundings. Like most such places, it offered food and drink in addition to rooms for the night. There were only a few customers at this time of the day. A sky pilot perched on a stool at the counter, exchanging war stories with the ebony-skinned man behind the bar. A couple of local farmers shared a table near the door, a man and a woman huddled close together in a booth, apparently oblivious to everyone else.

Gryff led Marri to a booth in the back corner and slid in beside her, shielding her from the view of any casual observer.

"How long will it take us to reach Tarnn?" she asked.

He shrugged. "I'm not sure. I've never been there."

"But you know where it is? How to get there?"

"Don't worry, I'll find it."

A bored-looking waitress sauntered up to their booth. She took their order, winked at Gryff, and sashayed away.

"What's in Tarnn?" Gryff asked, his gaze lingering on the waitress's curvy behind.

"A place to hide."

He lifted one brow, waiting for her to go on. When she didn't, he said, "You're gonna have to tell me exactly where we're headed sooner or later if you want to get there."

"A cloister," she said.

"A cloister!" he repeated, his voice filled with disbelief. "You're gonna take holy vows?"

"Yes." Once she committed her life to the church, her brother would have no reason to come after her. And though she didn't really want to spend the rest of her life behind high stone walls, at least she would be safe from his treachery. And Annis would be there.

Gryff shook his head, wondering how such a lovely creature could even contemplate living a sequestered life. He knew all too well what it was like to be locked up. Just thinking about it filled him with despair. Sometimes he still had nightmares about the men he had killed in the arena. About the tiny cell where he had spent the majority of his time. The humiliation of being at Serepta's beck and call. The sting of the whip slicing into his flesh when he displeased her. The hot irons she had laid across his back and belly...

"Gryff? Gryff, are you all right?"

His head jerked up at the sound of his name. Marri was staring at him. "What?"

"Are you all right?" she asked again.

He took a deep breath, willing his heart to stop pounding. "Fine."

"You're hiding something, too, aren't you?" she asked candidly.

The arrival of the waitress with their food spared him the need to answer, at least for the moment.

Marri stared out the side window of the skiff. They had driven for miles, yet the scenery never changed - brown dirt, brown plants. The land was arid and mostly uninhabited. Once, they passed a dilapidated space port. Such places were usually busy; this one had been virtually empty.

Closing her eyes, she tried to sleep, but sleep wouldn't come. Instead, she recalled the events of the last few days before she had met Gryff. She remembered the fear that had engulfed her when she woke up in a small room and realized she was a prisoner with no memory of who she was. She recalled hitting one of the men over the head with a chair and squeezing out of a tiny, narrow window. She didn't remember anything after that until she lifted her head from the bar in the tavern and saw Gryff staring down at her.

She slid a glance in his direction. Not for the first time, she wondered how he had known about the two men the wolf had killed, and where the blood on his hands had come from if it wasn't his. Had the wolf been a pet? She dismissed that idea as soon as it occurred to her. If the wolf was a pet, wouldn't Gryff have brought it with him?

With a sigh, she closed her eyes again.

Gryff eased the kinks out of his back and shoulders. They had traveled about five hours since leaving his place. It would be dark soon. Night fell quickly at this time of the year. They needed to find a safe haven to spend the night.

An hour later, he found a suitable place to park the skiff. The woman was still asleep and he saw no reason to wake her. Climbing out of the vehicle, he circled around to the back and opened the hatch. A light came on as he stepped into the cabin. Gryff shook his head as he glanced at the interior—a pair of narrow cots covered with well-worn blankets, a small metal table, two metal benches, a cold storage compartment, and a heating element. A tiny lavatory with a toilet and small sink took up space in the far corner. There was a closet the size of a shoebox next to the lavatory, a tank that held drinking water. Newer, more expensive models came equipped with entertainment cubes, kitchens, and bedrooms.

He had ordered a couple of meals to go from the tavern. Removing them from the carry sacks, he tossed the trays into the heating element and hit the timer. Leaving them to heat, he went back to the front of the craft to wake Marri.

"Hey." He shook her shoulder gently. "Wake up."

She woke with a start, her eyes wide with fear. "Don't!"

"Easy, princess."

She glanced around. "Is something wrong?"

"No, we're gonna spend the night here. Come on," he said, step-ping away from the door. "Dinner's ready."

She followed him to the back of the skiff, paused at the hatch when he stepped inside.

"Come on in," Gryff said. "It's not much, but it'll keep you warm and dry."

It was with a great deal of trepidation that she entered the craft. The living quarters of the skiff were reminiscent of the shack, save that the shack had been a little bigger.

Gryff jerked his chin toward the small table located midway be-tween the front of the cabin and the rear. "Sit down."

With some reluctance, she sat on the edge of one of the grimy benches, watching in silence as he dropped two covered plates on the table before sitting across from her.

Removing the cover from his plate, he began to eat.

Marri stared at the food in front of her. Like everything else in this godforsaken land, it was mostly brown. What was she doing here, in this place, with this man? It was like a horrible dream that kept getting worse.

Picking up her fork, she took a bite, though she hardly tasted what she ate. She was tired and homesick and afraid. She wanted a bath. She wanted to wear her own clothes. She wanted to sleep in her own bed. She wanted her life back.

She looked up to find Gryff watching her. "Is something wrong?" she asked.

He shook his head. "I was just wondering who you really are and why your brother wants to kill you."

"Because he's insane," she retorted. "I don't think sane people kill their siblings, do you?"

"Siblings?"

Marri looked away. The man didn't miss a thing. She hadn't meant to let that slip out. She would have to be more careful in the future.

"Who else did he kill?" Gryff asked.

"No one."

He lifted one brow, tacitly calling her a liar once again.

"I can't prove that he killed anyone, but I…" She had felt her brothers die, but, fearing that no one would believe her, or that they would think she was some kind of sorceress, she had never men-tioned it to anyone. Though sorely tempted to tell Gryff everything, she resisted. She was afraid to trust him, afraid to trust anyone. Someone had drugged her morning tea. Artur wanted her dead. The fact that he had sent his assassins after her proved that, even if she couldn't prove anything else.

Gryff ate the last of his meager meal, then lit a cigarette.

Marri wrinkled her nose against the smell. She had never known anyone who smoked. She glanced at his scars, wondering how he had gotten them. After a few minutes, her curiosity overcame her manners.

"Were you in a fight?" she asked, gesturing at the scar on his cheek.

He grunted softly. "More of them than I care to remember."

"Why? Don't people like you?"

He laughed, but there was no humor in the sound, or in the way his eyes narrowed.

"It wasn't my choice."

"They why do it?"

"Like I said, it wasn't my choice."

She frowned. "I don't understand."

He looked at her for a long moment while he decided whether to tell her about his past or not. Muttering, "What the hell," he took a deep drag on his cigarette, then stared at the glowing end. "I was a slave," he said, his voice bitter. "I spent five years in an underground cage, fighting in the arena to please my mistress."

He watched Marri's eyes, those beautiful blue-green eyes, widen in horror. "Who…where?" She shook her head. "How awful that must have been!"

"You have no idea." Had a mere mortal captured him, he could have escaped with ease, but Serepta was no mere mortal.

She had been blessed with magical powers. Not satisfied with magic alone, she had sought the Dark Gift, which turned her into a vampyre. The combination of witchcraft and preternatural power made her invincible. She had captured beings from all over the galaxy and matched them against each other in her underground arena. Gryff had fought men and women — human and inhuman - from other planets once a week, sometimes more often, for five long years. The winners had lived to fight another day. Serepta had other uses for the losers who survived.

In the beginning, fighting had been a way to release his anger, his frustration at being caged like a wild animal. Serepta had loved it best when he fought in wolf form, when he savaged his opponent with teeth and claws. The sight and scent of fresh blood excited her, as did the sounds of men in torment. On those nights when she didn't have a suitable match for him, she chained him to a post and whipped him until his back was raw, until, in spite of his determination to resist, he had cried out in agony. And then, with his back raw and bleeding, she licked the blood from his flesh. Her saliva healed his wounds, but the touch of her tongue on his skin was even more painful than the bite of the lash. As bad as those nights had been, the nights when she had chained him to her bed had been worse.

"Gryff?"

He looked up. Lost in the past, he had forgotten Marri was there.

"Are you all right?"

"Sure. Why don't you turn in? We'll be on our way again at first light."

She looked at him a moment, her eyes filled with sympathy, and then she took off her shoes and slid, fully-clothed, into the nearest bunk.

Gryff stared out the window. He could feel the woman watching him. What would she think if she knew how bad it had really been? Would she look at him with the same revulsion he felt for what he had done, for the lives he had ruined to preserve his own? Serepta had vowed he would never escape her. He feared she was right. Even if he destroyed her, he would still bear the scars she had inflicted on his mind and his body.

Clad in nothing but a loincloth, he stood with his feet braced, his arms drawn up as far as they would go, his wrists tightly manacled to a bar over his head. Behind him, he heard Serepta flicking the whip, its snake-like hiss warning him of the pain to come. Dread coiled deep in his gut. His hands clenched into fists, his whole body tense as he waited. And waited. Damn and blast, what was she waiting for? Why didn't she just get it over with? Sweat beaded across his brow, dripped into his eyes. Damn! He stared at the far wall, concentrating on how much he hated her, imagining all the ways he would kill her if he could just get his hands on her.

Soft laughter filled the air. And then the whip curled around his body, singing a familiar song of pain. He gasped, surprised as always that anything could hurt so much. And yet it wasn't just the pain that made him cringe. It was the humiliation of standing there, helpless and at her mercy. Soon, he knew that he would give voice to the agony she inflicted, knew he would promise to do whatever she asked if she would only lay the whip aside…

Gryff swore under his breath and the images receded. Would he ever be free of her? Of the shame and humiliation? There had been days, weeks, when she forced him to remain in his wolf form. She had treated him like a pet hound, forcing him sit at her side, compelling him to sleep on the floor at the foot of her bed. She had taken him outside and made him hunt rabbits so she could have a new fur cloak. She conjured a magical collar that had no lock and no key. It was an amazing piece of work, in that it obeyed her commands. At her word, it wrapped around his neck. At her word, it fell away. At her whim, it prevented him from shifting from man to wolf, or wolf to man. It also had the power to inflict pain so intense as to render him momentarily helpless. And then, to make certain he couldn't run away in either form, she conjured a magical chain that extended or retracted at her will even as it had kept him under her control.

He rubbed his hand over his neck. Even now, months later, he could feel the weight of that accursed collar.

With a sigh, he looked over at the woman. She was sleeping peacefully, her cheek resting on her hand. Her hair spread over the pillow like a splash of gold ink, her eyelashes rested like fans of silk against her cheeks. Just looking at her calmed the storm within him. He wished he had the right to crawl in beside her and take her in his arms, to hold her close, stroke her hair, feel the softness of her skin beneath his hand.

He hadn't made love to a woman in over five years. He had pleasured Serepta, but it hadn't been love, nor had he ever gone willingly to her bed.

He swore softly, his bile rising with the memory. How he hated her! But no more than he hated himself.

"Gryff?" Marri's voice, sleep soft. "Gryff, are you all right?"

"Sure. Go back to sleep." He heard the bed creak and then she was there in the dark beside him.

"Do you want to talk about it?"

He grunted softly, remembering that he had spoken the same words to her not so long ago. "No."

She placed a tentative hand on his shoulder. "I'd like to help," she murmured.

The warmth of her touch penetrated his shirt, warming the skin beneath, arrowing straight down to his groin. "Why?"

"Because you're helping me."

"Thanks, but there's nothing you can do."

With a sigh, she drew his head to her breast and after a moment, she lightly stroked his hair.

Her touch, filled with a gentleness and compassion that he hadn't felt in years, was his undoing. With a sob, his arms went around her waist. He clung to her like a child afraid of the dark while hot tears stung his eyes and burned his cheeks.

She murmured to him, soft meaningless words of solace and comfort as she lightly massaged his neck and back.

Under other circumstances, it might have relaxed him, but it had been years since he had been with a woman he desired. Every indrawn breath carried her scent to him, every touch of her hand fueled his desire.

He swore softly. It was bad enough that he was behaving like a frightened child. If he didn't put some space between them, in another minute he would have her flat on her back beneath him.

Muttering another oath, he drew back. He couldn't look at her, couldn't face the disdain he was sure to see in her eyes. He was a grown man. He was supposed to be looking after her, not acting like an mewling infant, or some wild, rutting beast. He didn't know which shamed him more, his tears or his lust.

Still not looking at her, he muttered, "I'm sorry."

"It's all right," she said quietly. "Good night."

He heard the bunk creak beneath her weight as she climbed onto the bed, the soft whisper of cloth against cloth as she slid under the covers and turned her back to him.

Damn and blast. He didn't know how he was ever going to face her again.

Marri stared into the darkness, the bodice of her dress still damp from Gryff's tears. She couldn't believe she had comforted him while he cried. Found it hard to believe he was capable of tears. He seemed so strong and self-assured, beyond emotions like sorrow or regret. Her palm tingled when she recalled how she had stroked his hair. Consoling him had seemed like the most natural thing in the world.

She couldn't remember ever comforting anyone who wasn't a member of her family. She had been acutely aware that Gryff wasn't one of her brothers. His masculine scent had teased her senses, the weight of his head against her breast had sent shivers of awareness spiraling through her, made her think of things she had never considered before, made her yearn to slip her hands under his shirt and feel his bare skin beneath her palms, to press his body to hers, to touch him and taste him.

Heat flooded her cheeks. What was wrong with her? Why was she having these strange feelings about a man she hardly knew?

She turned onto her stomach and slid a surreptitious glance in his direction. He sat at the table staring out the window, a smoldering cigarette in his hand. He looked dark and dangerous and alone, she thought. So alone. She wondered suddenly if he was married. But surely not. He had never mentioned a wife. He wore no ring.

With a sigh, she closed her eyes. Sleep, she thought. It was the best thing for her. She heard the sound of the cabin door opening. Gryff, she thought, probably going outside to stretch his legs before he went to bed.

Moments later, just as she was drifting off, she thought she heard the melancholy howl of a wolf.

The wolf ran wild in the night, feet flying across the ground, nostrils absorbing and filtering a thousand scents. He was aware of other animals in the underbrush, heard the high-pitched squeal that signaled another midnight hunter had caught its prey. But the wolf wasn't in search of prey, he was running for the sheer love of it, running because it had been denied him for so long. Running as if he could run from his past.

Freedom!

He soared effortlessly over a fallen log, felt a rush of excitement as he chased a wild hare. He heard the panicked beat of the frightened creature's heart and veered off to the left. He didn't kill for sport, only when he was hungry.

He drank in the wind, reveled in its touch on his face and in the feel of the earth beneath the pads of his feet. The thrill of being free welled up within him and he howled his joy into the night.

The cry of another wolf reached his ears and he slowed to a stop, ears twitching as he sought the source. It had been years since he had run with the wild ones. The melancholy cry came again and he started off in that direction, only to come to an abrupt halt.

As much as he yearned to run with his wild cousins, it would have to wait for another time. He had left the woman alone long enough.

The howling of wolves woke her. Sitting up in bed, Marri looked at the other bunk. Empty. Gryff must still be outside.

Sitting up, she glanced out the cabin's narrow window. Fear knotted in her stomach. She told herself there was nothing to be afraid of, that the wolves couldn't possibly get inside the Landskiff. She had nothing to fear.

The hair raised along the back of her neck as another howl broke the quiet of the night. This one was closer. Too close.

Leaning forward, she peered into the darkness. There! Something was moving out there. She pressed a hand to her heart. If only Gryff were here, she wouldn't be afraid. But he hadn't returned and she was alone. And there was someone, or something, moving outside, in the shadows.

She told herself again there was nothing to be afraid of. As long as she stayed inside the craft, she was safe.

Her breath caught in her throat as the creature stepped out of the shadows and into a ray of moonlight.

"Gryff." His name whispered past her lips even as shock rippled through her.

Marri knew she should avert her eyes, but she couldn't seem to move. She could understand a man wanting to go outside for a smoke or for a few minutes of fresh air, but why was he naked?

CHAPTER 6

Marri knew she should turn away or lower her gaze eyes but she couldn't stop staring at him. She had never seen a naked man before, and this one was beautiful, from his broad shoulders and hard, flat stomach to his long, muscular legs and muddy feet. His skin was a deep golden brown, all over. Overhead, Brynn Tor's twin winter moons shone brightly, revealing him in all his glorious masculinity. Only gradually did she become aware of the thick spider web of silvery scars that marred the perfection of his arms and legs and criss-crossed his chest and back. So many scars. She supposed they were souvenirs of the arena, yet they looked like marks left by the lash. Of course, she thought. Hadn't he told her he had been a slave?

She gasped and drew away from the window when he looked her way. Had he seen her staring at him? The very thought brought a rush of heat to her cheeks. And yet she couldn't resist the urge to look again, couldn't contain her disappointment when she looked and he was gone.

The sound of the hatch opening filled her with a rush of guilt. How could she face him when he knew she had been watching him?

Maybe he hadn't seen her! After all, it was dark inside the cabin. She slid quickly under the covers, turned her back to the door, and closed her eyes, willing herself to take slow, deep breaths.

She heard the soft slap of his bare feet as he walked toward the back of the cabin. She knew he was standing beside her bed. The sweep of his gaze was a palpable thing. Breathe, she thought. Slowly. In. Out. In. Out.

It seemed he stood there for an eternity before she heard the creak of the opposite bunk as he settled down for the night.

Gryff folded his arms behind his head and stared up at the ceiling. He knew the woman was awake, knew the moment she drifted off to sleep. She had seen him emerge from the wild. Her gaze had been almost tangible as she watched him through the window. For a moment, he had closed his eyes and imagined her hands moving over his skin, her fingertips lightly caressing him, her lips tasting him. He wondered how he was going to explain being naked in the moonlight. He didn't owe her any explanations, he thought with a shrug. Nor could he deny the rush of desire that had engulfed him when he felt her gaze on him. He grinned into the darkness, thinking she had probably seen a lot more than she bargained for. Then again, maybe not. She had three brothers, after all.

He glanced across the narrow aisle that separated her bunk from his. Her scent filled the air, subtle, feminine, ripe. For one brief moment, he considered the unthinkable. He could slide into the bunk beside her and ease the ache her nearness aroused. He could keep her for himself until he tired of her and then take her home.

He muttered a vile oath, disgusted that, after what he had endured at Serepta's hands, he could even consider such a thing.

Turning his back to her, he closed his eyes and forced himself to think about the route they would take tomorrow. It wouldn't be an easy journey. There were cutthroats and robbers between here and the next town. With any luck, the storm he sensed would arrive before morning and keep the thugs in their holes.

At daybreak, they ate a quick breakfast, then left the cabin. After making sure the woman was safely settled in her seat, Gryff fired up the skiff's engine. Overhead, lightning forked through the lowering clouds.

He couldn't help noticing that she kept as much distance between them as possible. Nor did he miss the surreptitious glances she cast his way once they were on the road. He grinned inwardly, amused and somewhat flattered. Maybe she wasn't as upset by what she had seen the night before as he supposed.

"So, princess," he said as the skiff leveled out, "why don't you tell me about yourself? You married? Betrothed?"

"No."

It was obvious that she wasn't in the mood to talk, leastwise not about herself. Or maybe just not to him.

"Gonna be a mighty long, quiet trip, girl, if you won't talk to me," he remarked.

She shrugged.

"How about this? I ask you a question. You answer, and then you ask me a question. Where I come from, we call that conversation."

Stifling a grin, she smoothed a wrinkle from her skirt. "Are you married?"

"No. Not now, not ever."

"What do you have against marriage?" she asked.

"Nothing. It's just not for me. My turn. Why does your brother want to kill you?"

"He thinks I want something that he feels should rightfully be his."

"And you don't want it?"

"No. That's why I'm going to Tarnn. Aren't you going to get in trouble for leaving your job?"

He shrugged. "I'm not afraid of trouble." He slid a glance in her direction, his gaze moving over her in a way that made Marri's toes curl. "If I was, I wouldn't be with you."

"What does that mean?"

"I can smell trouble a mile away, honey, and you reek of it from the top of your pretty red head to the soles of your feet."

Lips drawn in a tight line, she gave him a decidedly dirty look. "I have nothing more to say to you."

With a shrug, he turned his attention back to the road.

Marri folded her arms over her chest, determined not to speak to him again. She didn't mean to cause him trouble. After all, it wasn't her fault that her brother wanted her dead. And if Gryff didn't want her around, then he shouldn't have offered to take her to Tarnn.

Several silent miles passed.

"Did you get all those scars in the arena?" she asked abruptly. Too late, she realized she had just admitted to spying on him the night before.

He looked over at her, an amused expression in his deep brown eyes.

Heat climbed up her neck and into her cheeks. Mortified, she looked out the window again.

Silence again stretched between them. Marri chewed on her thumbnail. Maybe she should tell him everything. What difference would it make if he knew who she was? The immediate and obvious answer was: a big difference! He could demand a ransom from her father, or worse, from her brother. Her only protection was to keep him in the dark as to her real identity. Once they reached the abbey, she would be safe and she would never see him, or any other man, again.

It was mid-morning when he stopped at a small tavern so they could get something to eat.

When Gryff opened the door, every eye in the place turned in their direction. Suddenly uneasy, Marri pressed close to his side. Never in all her life had she seen such a group of rough-looking men. Most had shaggy beards and unkempt hair. And feral eyes that seemed to bore into her. She was certain they would as soon slit her throat—or worse—as look at her.

Gryff gestured to an empty booth near the front. Marri slid over by the window, and he slid in beside her.

Marri kept her gaze fixed on her folded hands. All those disreputable men staring at her made her feel dirty.

"Marri, what do you want to eat?"

"Anything," she said, not looking up.

Gryff ordered steak, fries, and coffee for both of them.

When their meal came, Marri kept her gaze on her plate, hardly aware of what she was eating. All she wanted to do was get out of there, the sooner, the better.

Gryff ordered coffee and sandwiches to go and paid the check. He handed the take-out sack to Marri, then followed her out the door, one hand on the knife sheathed beneath his jacket.

She breathed a sigh of relief when they stepped outside. She had just opened the door of the skiff when she heard loud voices behind her.

Glancing over her shoulder, she saw that three men had followed them out of the café. One was tall with dark skin, the second was thin and wiry, the third perhaps an inch taller than Gryff.

"Get inside and lock the door," Gryff said from behind her.

She quickly did as bidden, then peered out the window.

The three men surrounded Gryff, taunting him about what they would do to his woman after they finished with him.

She sucked in a deep breath when she saw the flash of sunlight on steel. Three against one. What chance did Gryff have?

She watched in awe as he parried the trio's thrusting blades. Whirling, ducking, jabbing, he moved with a feral grace she had never seen before.

It was exciting, exhilarating. Frightening.

What would she do if he lost the fight?

But he wasn't losing. Even as she watched, he slit the throat of the man nearest him. The man went down amid a spray of crimson, convulsed, and lay still. A second man met a similar fate when Gryff's blade slid between his ribs. The man fell to his knees; then, hands pressed against the killing wound, he pitched forward and lay still.

Marri watched in horror as Gryff and the third man circled one another. Knees bent, chins tucked in, arms outstretched, they slashed at each other in a silent dance of death. She couldn't take her gaze from Gryff. Eyes narrowed, teeth bared, his face and body splattered with blood, he was the most frightening, fascinating being she had ever seen.

Her breath caught in her throat when the tall man's blade opened a long gash in Gryff's left arm. Gryff went down on one knee, and then, almost quicker than her eye could follow, he feinted left, dodged right. With a wild cry that reminded her of a wolf's howl, he plunged his knife into his opponent's belly and jerked it upward.

Choking back the bile that rose in her throat, Marri closed her eyes, sickened by the sight of the man's intestines spilling out like fat pink worms.

She heard the driver's side door open as Gryff climbed into the Landskiff, felt the craft lurch forward. Who was this man sitting beside her that he could dispatch three attackers so skillfully, who killed so efficiently?

Whoever he was, she was glad he was on her side.

Opening her eyes, she glanced at him. While watching the battle, she had been so intent on the fight, she hadn't realized he had received so many wounds besides the one on his arm. Now, a wordless cry of alarm rose in her throat when she noticed the many dark stains spreading across his shirt and trousers. "You're bleeding everywhere!"

He grunted softly.

She stared at the blood soaking his clothing, at the gash on his arm, the cut on his left shoulder. "Your arm needs stitching. Shouldn't we find a doctor?"

"I don't think that would be a very smart thing to do."

"Who were those men?"

"I don't know. Maybe just drifters." Or maybe Serepta's henchmen. Forcing that disconcerting thought aside, he slanted a glance in Marri's direction. "Maybe your brother's assassins."

She didn't want to think about that. "Well, shouldn't we at least stop and bandage your wounds before you bleed to death?"

"Yeah, I reckon so," he agreed, though it wasn't really necessary. Some of his minor injuries were already healing. Still, he needed to let her tend the others. She'd think it strange if he told her it wasn't necessary.

Marri braced herself as the skiff bumped its way along a road that grew bumpier and narrower with each passing mile.

She was about to ask Gryff if he knew where the path ended when he pulled up underneath a tall tree and switched off the engine.

"Where are we?" she asked.

"Nowhere." Opening the door, he got out of the vehicle and made his way around to the hatch.

Marri glanced out the windows, making sure there were no animals lurking in the bushes before she followed him to the rear of the skiff.

Gryff was already inside. He had removed his shirt and she saw that he had sustained even more cuts and gashes than she had thought. In addition to several deep knife wounds, there were a number of small cuts and shallow gashes across his back and shoulders.

"Do you have any bandages?" she asked, stepping inside and closing the door behind her.

"I don't know." He sat down on one of the benches. "Check the drawers and see what you can find."

He didn't know? She thought it odd that he didn't know what supplies he had onboard. Searching through the drawers, she found an unmatched set of silverware, a box of matches, a flashlight, a deck of playing cards, several towels and washcloths, a can of antibacterial spray, and a couple of faded shirts. No bandages. She put the antiseptic on the table, then looked at Gryff.

"Hand me one of those shirts," he said. "then soak one of those towels in cold water and bring it here."

While he tore the shirt into strips, she did as he'd asked, picked up the soap, threw a second towel over her shoulder, and then, taking a deep breath, she knelt in front of him. The wound in his left arm seemed to be bleeding the most, so she started there.

A muscle throbbed in his jaw when she began washing the blood from the wound.

When she finished cleaning the injury, she patted his skin dry, sprayed the cut with antiseptic, then bandaged it with one of strips he had torn from the shirt.

Marri tried not to notice how well-muscled he was as she washed the blood spattered across his chest and shoulders. The cuts here were mostly superficial, as was the one across his back. All had stopped bleeding by the time she had him cleaned up.

Muttering, "Thanks," he stood. Taking one of the shirts from the drawer, he tugged it over his head. It was a tight fit, but it was relatively clean.

"Let's go."

Marri glanced out the window at the never-changing landscape. They had been traveling for several hours, stopping only for a meager lunch of meat and cheese. She was hungry and tired and, though she was loath to admit it, afraid of what lay ahead? What if the nuns refused to admit her? Lost in thought, she closed her eyes.

When she woke, the night was as black as the ebony caves of Brynn Tor. She glanced at Gryff, wondering why they had stopped.

"We're spending the night here," he explained.

Marri looked out the window. "Here?" she asked tremulously.

"You know a better place?"

She shook her head.

When he got out of the skiff, she followed him around to the back.

Opening the cabin door, he gestured for her to get inside. "I'm gonna go have a look around."

"Do you have to?"

"'Fraid so. Lock the door."

With a nod, she did as she was told, then looked out the window, but there was no sign of Gryff. How could he have disappeared so quickly?

Filled with nervous tension, she picked up his blood-stained shirt, wondering if she should try to mend it or just throw it away.

She was still debating when a wolf's howl cut through the stillness of the night.

CHAPTER 7

Gryff ran through the darkness, the pain of his wounds forgotten in the sheer ecstasy of embracing his wolf form and feeling himself one with the night. But no matter how far he ran, he couldn't outrun the memory of the woman waiting for him in the skiff, couldn't forget the worry in her eyes, the warmth and tenderness of her hands as she bathed his wounds. The scent of her hair. The almost velvety softness of her skin.

Nor could he outrun the sudden, inexplicable urge to find a life mate.

He had coupled with Serepta because he had no choice in the matter. He had performed the act of mating, nothing more. With his true mate, it would have been deeply meaningful—a joining of more than flesh, a fusion of heart and soul, of mind and spirit.

Right or wrong, impossible or not, he wanted Marri to be his woman, his life mate. He had known it from the moment he first saw her, just as he had known it was like wishing for the moon.

He paused beneath a tree. Even if she was the right woman, even if she accepted him, there was no chance for them now, not with the threat of Serepta's wrath hanging over his head. And then there was the matter of Marri's mysterious brother. Who was she? And why did her brother really want her dead?

With a yelp, he put all human worries from his mind and raced through the night. For the wolf, there was no past, no future. There was only now, the freedom of the night.

He lifted his head as lightning forked through the clouds, followed by the rumble of thunder and the soft patter of rain.

Marri glanced at Gryff as he pulled onto the main road, now awash in mud. Last night, she had waited up for him as long as she could, curious to know where he had gone, but sleep claimed her before he returned. So she put the question to him now. "Where did you go last night?"

He shrugged. "Just out for some fresh air."

"In the rain?"

He shrugged again.

"I didn't see you when I looked out the window."

"It was dark."

"Not that dark."

"Maybe you need glasses."

Marri glared at him. Glasses, indeed. He had stepped out of the craft and disappeared into the night as if he was a part of it. And why was it that every time he went outside, she heard a wolf's howl? Was that big black wolf she had seen back at his place following them?

It was late afternoon when Gryff pulled the skiff to a stop. There was a town ahead. Thus far, he had avoided space ports, but Bosquetown was the only settlement for the next six hundred miles. They hadn't eaten since last night. They were out of food, out of water.

"Why are we stopping?" Marri asked.

"I need a break." He jerked his head toward the space port that shimmered in the distance. "I need a break and a drink," he muttered, "and something to eat. How about you?"

Marri nodded, then blushed when her stomach took that moment to make a very un-ladylike rumble.

Well, shit, he couldn't let her starve. "Bosquetown, it is," he muttered.

Like most of the space ports this side of Brynn Tor, this one was little more than a few ramshackle buildings. He glanced at the call board beside the entrance, relieved when he didn't find a flyer with his face on it.

Since it was too early for dinner and too late for lunch, the restaurant was empty save for one burly pilot sitting at the counter, a cup of coffee in one hand, a cigar in the other.

Gryff led the way to a table in the back. Once they were settled, he handed Marri one of the menus before picking up the second.

He had just decided on steak and eggs when a sudden uneasiness sent a warning chill down his spine. Before he could locate the cause of his unrest, he felt a sharp prick in the back of his neck, and then he felt nothing at all.

Marri screamed as Gryff collapsed onto the table. She stared at him, wondering what she would do, when two men materialized, seemingly out of nowhere. One of them wrapped his arm around her neck and held her immobile while the second man shackled Gryff's hands behind his back. She watched in disbelief as the stranger pressed what looked like a strip of solid gold against Gryff's neck, gasped as the metal encircled his throat, the ends meeting and somehow melding together. With the collar in place, the guard dragged Gryff out of the booth, hefted him onto his shoulder, and carried him out of the tavern.

Marri glanced around, praying for someone to help them, but no one paid any attention when the man holding her dragged her away.

Outside, her hands were bound in front of her and she was shoved into the cargo hold of a large transport. Gryff lay motionless on the floor. A thick chain had been attached to the collar around his neck, tethering him to a stout iron ring set in the metal floor of the transport.

Marri jumped as one of the men shut and locked the door. Moments later, the vehicle lurched forward.

She stared into the darkness that surrounded her. Her worst nightmare had come true. Artur had found her.

Gryff regained consciousness with a low groan. Cracking one eye open, he stared into the darkness. When he tried to sit up, he discovered that his hands were shackled behind his back.

He swore softly. He didn't know how, but Serepta had found him. Her threat echoed in his mind, sending shivers of terror down his spine. *I will find you and flay the flesh from your bones an inch at a time*, she had vowed. *And then I will heal you and do it again.*

He rolled onto his knees, his terror increasing when he felt the familiar weight of the gold collar around his neck and realized he was chained to the floor. He gathered his strength, then called upon his power, but nothing happened. The collar was working.

"Gryff, are you awake?"

Her voice seemed to come from far away. "Marri?"

"I'm here."

"Are you all right?"

"Yes. Are you?"

"Yeah, sure," he muttered. "I'm just great."

She felt around in the dark until her hand touched his thigh. "I'm sorry I got you into this."

"You didn't get me into anything."

"Of course I did. If it wasn't for me, you wouldn't be here now."

"You've got it all wrong, sweetheart. If it wasn't for me, *you* wouldn't be here."

"I don't understand."

"You're not the only one on the run." Though he couldn't see more than a vague outline, he knew she was staring at him, waiting for him to explain. "Your brother's after you. I've got a witch after me."

"A witch!" she exclaimed.

"Yeah. Remember I told you I'd been a slave? Well, Serepta was my mistress, damn her black soul to hell."

"How do you know she's behind this?"

"The collar around my neck. I recognize it from the last time."

"What will she do now?"

I will find you and flay the flesh from your bones an inch at a time.

He shook his head. "I don't even want to think about it." Inflicting pain was Serepta's favorite pastime and she was nothing if not inventive.

Marri sat back on her heels. She had been terrified to think that her brother's men had found her but she had a horrible feeling that she would have been better off with Artur than with Gryff's witch.

Lost in darkness, she had no sense of time passing. It could have been hours later, it could have been minutes, before the transport came to a stop. She huddled against Gryff, her fear growing with each beat of her heart. No matter whose hands they had fallen into, the future for both of them looked bleak at best.

The door of the transport opened with an eerie creak. A man appeared in the opening. He tossed a sack inside, dropped a container of water on the floor, and closed the door, leaving them in darkness once again.

Drawn by the scent of food, Marri crawled toward the sack, feeling her way with her hands. It took several minutes to find the water. Carrying the sack in her teeth and the water bottle in her cupped hands, she inched her way back to Gryff.

Dropping the bag, she delved inside. "Are you hungry?" She withdrew a round of cheese and several slabs of meat. "Do you think it's safe to eat?"

Gryff snorted softly. "She didn't hunt me down just to poison me."

Marri offered him a slice of meat, alternately feeding him and herself until the meat and cheese were gone and the water container was empty.

A short time later, the transport lurched forward.

Marri huddled in the darkness. She tried not to think of what might await them at the end of their journey, but numerous scenarios chased themselves across her mind, none of them pleasant. A witch. The very word sent a chill down her spine. Her father had hired hunters to expel the witches from Brynn Tor, and destroyed any who refused to leave. Needless to say, the witch population had not been happy about that, which was why her father had summoned Nardik. He was a powerful wizard, the only being she knew who had power stronger than a witch's. At her father's command, Nardik had cast a spell to protect Brynn Tor and its inhabitants from harmful magic. She only wished Nardik was with her now, but he had left the castle shortly after her mother disappeared.

She felt a surge of alarm when the transport shuddered to a halt. Had they reached their destination?

She pressed close to Gryff as the door swung open and four hooded men climbed inside.

One of them grabbed her by the arm and dragged her out of the vehicle. She was surprised to see that night had fallen.

"Rest stop," the man said, his voice little more than a growl.

She was stretching her arms and shoulders when Gryff stepped out of the transport. Two men flanked him, the third held the chain. It was then that she noticed all the men were heavily armed with blasters and stunners.

Three of the men led Gryff into a stand of timber, leaving the fourth man to keep an eye on her.

Gryff made his way into the cover of the trees, wondering if they intended to kill him. He dismissed the idea as quickly as it formed. If he was to die, he was certain that Serepta would want to be there to deliver the killing blow herself.

The three men guarding him relieved themselves. One of them freed Gryff's hands so that he, too, could answer nature's call. Had it not been for the collar around his neck, he would have made a break for it, but there was no way to escape as long as they held the chain.

When his hands were again shackled behind his back, they marched him to the transport. One of the guards thrust a bottle of water into Marri's hands and then he and Marri were herded into the vehicle. When the chain was secured to the iron ring in the floor, the prisoners were left in darkness.

"It's a long way to Serepta's lair," Gryff remarked. "You might as well get some sleep." "What about you?" she asked.

"I'm not tired."

Feeling her way in the dark, Marri stretched out beside him, her head pillowed on his lap.

Moments later, she was asleep.

Gryff stared into the darkness, his thoughts as black as his surroundings as the transport sped through the night, carrying him ever closer to Serepta and the lingering, excruciating punishment she had promised him.

Chapter 8

"Gryff?"

"I thought you were asleep?"

"I was, for a little while." Rubbing her eyes, Marri sat up. "I've been wondering, how did you escape from Serepta the last time?"

How had he escaped? Gryff thought back to that time that seemed so long ago, yet it seemed like only yesterday that he had been Serepta's pet. She had kept him close night and day, rarely letting him out of her sight. When activated, the heavy collar thwarted his ability to change shape. When he was in human form, she kept him chained at her bedside, the better to pleasure her when she was in the mood. When in his wolf form, she kept him shackled to the wall in her bedroom, or, more often, locked in a cage. In spite of her supernatural powers, she had never trusted him when he was in wolf form. And rightly so. Given the chance, he would have ripped out her heart.

But one night…ah, that one night. She had been insatiable and he had pleasured her for hours. Finally exhausted, she had shortened his tether and chained him to the wall across from her bed . But that night, ah, that blessed night she had forgotten to activate the collar. Perhaps she had not forgotten, but assumed that he would not be able to escape the blasted thing even if he shifted into the wolf, since he was a very large wolf and the collar was very tight.

But he had not shifted into his wolf form. Instead, he had shifted into a small dog—an ability of which Serepta had been unaware—and slipped out of the collar. Regaining his own form, he fled her room and made his way to the keep's front door. A guard had tried to stop him but Gryff had shifted again.

The guard, though armed with a blaster, was no match for a large, angry wolf. Before the man could fire, Gryff launched himself at the guard and buried his fangs in his arm. The man dropped the weapon. With a feral growl, Gryff ripped out the man's throat and got the hell out of there just as fast as he could.

Drunk on freedom, he had taken off running and never looked back.

And now, too soon, he was her prisoner again.

Marri listened without interruption as Gryff told his story. It was fascinating. Intriguing. Unbelievable. "You were the wolf," she murmured. "You killed Dakkar and Trist."

"Yeah."

Marri shivered, unnerved by the thought. She was grateful for what he had done, yes, but…she had heard of shape-shifters but she had always believed they were creatures of fantasy. Now, if what Gryff said was true, they weren't creatures of myth at all.

Trying not to be obvious about it, she eased away from him.

"Are you afraid of me now?" he asked, one brow arching upward. "Afraid I might turn into a wild animal and gobble you up?"

"No." It sounded ridiculous, when he said it like that. But she couldn't forget he had killed Dakkar and Trist and torn the throat out of one of Serepta's guards.

"You're not much of a liar, are you?"

"That's what my brother always said."

"We're a fine pair," Gryff mused. "Your brother wants you dead. Serepta wants to torture me to the point of death and then do it all over again. Doesn't look like either one of us has much of a future."

A sudden chill crept over Marri. "What do think the witch will do with me? She won't send me back to Artur, will she?"

"You'd be better off if she did."

"Better off? He wants to kill me ."

"Believe me, dead is better than what Serepta has in mind for me."

"You're serious, aren't you?"

"Yeah. She told me if I ever escaped, she would flay the skin from my bones an inch at a time, then heal me and do it all again."

Marri shuddered at the image his words conjured in her mind. "She can do that?"

"Oh, yeah."

"And you escaped anyway?"

"Damn right. Whatever you do, don't tell her who you are. Your name is Cay. We met in Bosquetown. Got it?"

Before she could answer, the transport came to a jolting stop. Moments later, the door slid open. She couldn't really see anything other than a dark shape in the opening. A sudden flare of light illuminated a woman standing in the doorway. She held a staff in one hand, the tip of which provided the light.

Tall and regal, the woman had flawless porcelain skin, hair the color of cinnamon, and eyes as dark and cold as ebony.

Serepta.

She stepped into the transport, moving with a lithe grace. Her long black cloak flowed behind her. She paused in front of Gryff, her gaze frigid as she stared down at him.

He looked up at her, his own gaze defiant.

Then, slowly, Serepta turned her attention to Marri. "And who, pray tell, are you?"

"I'm…" She glanced at Gryff, who shook his head imperceptibly. "No one."

"You must have a name."

"Cay," she said. "I'm Cay."

Serepta lifted one brow, then summoned one of the guards. "Who is she? Why have you brought her here?"

"We don't know who she is, but they were together so…" He shrugged. "We brought her along."

Serepta nodded. "You did well. Take her to the dungeon and take him to my room." She looked down at Gryff, a cruel smile playing over her lips as she bent down to rake her nails over his cheek. "Strip him of his clothes and chain him to the wall." She glanced at the woman thoughtfully. "I've changed my mind. Take him to the dungeon, as well." Curling her fingers around a lock of his hair, she jerked his head back, forcing him to look up at her. "See you soon, wolf man."

Fear coiled deep in Gryff's belly as he watched her exit the transport. His worst nightmare was about to come true.

Marri curled up in the cleanest corner of her cell, her arms wrapped around her middle. She couldn't stop trembling. She was afraid, so afraid. Afraid for herself, but mostly afraid for Gryff. She could see him in the cell across the way. Serepta's guards had stripped him down to his loincloth. They had shackled his hands high over his head so that his feet barely touched the cold stone floor. The loose end of the chain attached to his collar was secured to an iron ring in the wall. The shackles around his ankles were chained to similar rings in the floor. It made her ache just to look at him—his body stretched painfully taut, every muscle sharply defined. Though sweat dripped down his back, he shivered convulsively. It might have been from the cold; she thought it more likely a bad case of nerves. He had to be afraid of what was coming. Had she been in his place, she would have been terrified.

The dungeon was silent save for the ticking of a clock, a distant drip of water, and the ragged rasp of Gryff's breathing.

She had never been inside a dungeon before. She knew there was one at home but her father had forbidden her to go there. She wondered if it was as cold and dreary as this one. The walls and floor were gray stone. There was no furniture in the cells for a straw tick on the floor and a smelly chamber pot in the corner. A single candle burned in a wrought iron sconce on the wall near the entrance. Its faint light did little to dispel the gloom.

A rustling in the tick drew Marri's attention. Grimacing, she pressed against the wall. She didn't know what lurked in the straw. She fervently hoped it wasn't a rat.

She had to get out of here, but how? For a moment, she considered telling Serepta the truth but that seemed a foolhardy thing to do. She didn't know what her fate would be at Serepta's hands, but she knew what fate awaited her at home. If she was going to die, she was glad it would be at the hands of a stranger. It would be less painful, she thought, than being betrayed and murdered by her own blood kin.

"Gryff?" Just saying his name made her feel better, though she had no idea why that should be. He couldn't help her now. No one could.

He grunted softly.

"I'm afraid." It was a silly thing to say. He knew she was afraid. They both were, but somehow it made her feel better. There was no shame in admitting it, after all. She hadn't been raised to be a warrior woman, but to be a wife and a mother. All her life, the ladies of the keep had looked after her. They had pampered her and spoiled her, taught her how to do needlepoint and dress her hair, how to greet guests and set a proper table. No one had thought to teach her how to defend herself from a witch.

She looked at Gryff again, wishing he could turn around so she could see his face. She longed to go to him, to put her arms around him and ease his pain, to dry the sweat that continued to drip down his neck, shoulders, and back.

She couldn't imagine what he was thinking, feeling, as he waited for Serepta. Dread coiled deep in her own belly at the mere thought of the fate that awaited him. She covered her mouth, choking back bitter bile as she realized that she would be there when it happened. She would hear the hiss of the whip, smell the blood, hear Gryff's anguished cries.

How would she bear it?

How could he?

Marri huddled in the corner, trying to make herself as small as possible, as the door to the dungeon opened with a hair-raising shriek.

And then Serepta appeared. A long black wool cloak covered a blood-red dress. In one hand, she carried her staff; in the other, a thick black whip.

Just looking at it made Marri shudder with revulsion. It was an instrument of exquisite torture, there was no doubt of that. Hoping to escape the witch's notice, Marri pressed deeper into the shadowy corner and closed her eyes.

At the sound of a key turning in the lock, Gryff's whole body stiffened with dreadful anticipation.

"So," Serepta said, her voice a hideous purr, "here we are, together again." She glided across the rough stones to caress his broad back. "It always seems a shame to mar such perfection."

Filled with dread at what was coming, he said nothing.

His hands curled into tight fists when he heard her shake out the whip. He knew that sound. It still haunted his dreams. She snapped it a few times, no doubt to remind him of the pain to come.

He flinched even before he felt the lash slither across his bare back. The pain never failed to surprise him. It was always worse than he remembered. His blood felt hot against the chill of his skin. He wondered if she had chosen to wear red so that his blood wouldn't show when it splattered over her gown.

She plied the whip again and yet again. He clamped his jaws together, determined not to cry out this time.

Four. Five. Six. His back was on fire, a solid sheet of flame that burned deep without consuming him. Blood flowed from the wounds, ran over his buttocks and down the backs of his legs. He heard Marri gasp each time Serepta plied the lash.

Coiling the whip, Serepta moved to stand in front of him. "Why do you make me do this?" She ran her fingers down his chest, the long, sharp nails leaving bloody furrows in their wake.

He shuddered at her touch.

She caressed his cheek, her expression thoughtful. "Did you miss me as much as I missed you?"

"Miss you?" He snorted softly. "Sure, I missed you, the way a hound misses its fleas."

Eyes blazing with anger, she slapped him. "You will not speak to me like that!"

"No? What more can you do to me?"

"I can let you die."

"Then why don't you?"

Serepta glared at him, and then she looked past him, her eyes narrowing thoughtfully. Abruptly, she turned on her heel and swept out of the cell.

Eyes closed, Gryff sagged against his bonds, grateful for the reprieve, until he heard Marri cry out in pain.

Groaning with the effort, he glanced over his shoulder to see Serepta chaining Marri's hands over her head.

"Serepta, no! Dammit, leave the girl alone."

Shaking out the whip, Serepta plied the lash in a sweeping arc. The leather ripped through cloth and flesh.

Marri screamed as the lash bit into her back.

Coiling the whip, Serepta returned to Gryff's cell where she kept her promise, whipping him until the flesh was flayed from his back and he hung limp in his chains, too weak to cry out. Standing there, her gown stained with his blood, she let him suffer for almost an hour before, with a murmured incantation, she healed his wounds.

Moving to stand in front of him, she cupped his chin in her hand, forcing him to look at her. "Who is the girl? What does she mean to you?"

"She's just a stray I picked up in Bosquetown. Said her name's Cay. She doesn't mean anything to me."

"We shall see. In the future, the girl will suffer for your disobedience and your insolence. Rest well, wolf man."

A flick of her hand extinguished the candle, and then she was gone.

Gryff took several deep breaths. "Marri? Marri, are you all right?"

She whimpered softly in reply.

Gryff swore under his breath. He could withstand whatever Serepta threw at him. He had endured five years of torture and humiliation at her hands, had tried time and again to escape in spite of the consequences because he had nothing to lose, but now…He swore again. Now, because of Marri, Serepta had him right where she wanted him. He would do whatever she asked. If he didn't, Marri would be the one to suffer for it.

Muttering an oath, he closed his eyes. Why was it, whenever he thought things couldn't get any worse, they always did?

CHAPTER 9

Artur paced the floor of his private chambers. Earlier that day, his father had announced that Artur would marry the Princess Kallen. Artur had known the alliance was coming. He knew the reason for it, but the thought of wedding and bedding the horse-faced princess of Sirrus was daunting. He had seen the wench only twice and been repulsed by her on both occasions. Neither her face nor her figure appealed to him. But, as his father had told him so many times in the past, an alliance with Sirrus was of far more importance than Artur's personal feelings on the matter.

With an eye on the lands and dowry Kallen would bring, Artur could hardly refuse. Once she had produced a male heir, and a second son as insurance should something befall the first, he would have no further use for her. Her demise would be easily arranged. A sudden, fatal illness, a fall from the tower window, a riding accident, perhaps, and he would be rid of her, free to marry a woman of his own choosing. Had Marri not been his kin, he would have chosen her…

Ah, Marri. She professed no interest in the throne, but history was rich with stories of men and women who denied they wished to rule and later changed their minds, wreaking havoc in the kingdom. Better to eliminate any and all potential rivals now. Her very presence would complicate things, especially if their father took it in his head to believe her suspicions about the deaths of Cobb and Caddin.

Moving to the mirror that stood in the corner, he stared at his reflection. "Soon," he murmured. "Soon, the kingdom will be mine."

As far back as he could remember, he had coveted the throne. As the youngest child in the family, he had always known that the only way he would ever obtain his heart's desire would be by force or deceit. Even then, he had discounted Marri. She was only a girl, after all. And Annis had early-on expressed her desire to take holy vows, sparing him the need to be rid of her.

It had infuriated him to know that Caddin was being groomed as the heir to the kingdom. Artur was wiser than both of his brothers, better suited to rule their holdings, and yet his father could not, or would not, see that his youngest son possessed qualities and leadership abilities that Caddin did not.

Artur slammed his fist against the wall. It had galled him that everyone in the kingdom had curried Caddin's favor. The young women of the court had fawned over him, hoping to gain favor with the future king.

When it became obvious to Artur that his father was too blind to see that Caddin lacked the wisdom to rule the kingdom, and that Cobb was more enamored of his mistress than power, Artur had taken matters into his own hands.

He turned his head this way and that, imagining his father's crown on his head. Marri was the only thing standing between himself and the throne. If Dunnin failed him, then, as distasteful as it might be, Artur would eliminate her himself.

Striding to the window, he cursed softly as he gazed out into the courtyard. Dunnin had been gone a fortnight without a word. Did Marri still live?

He turned as his mistress called his name. Ginna was a plump but pretty wench with fiery red hair and odd, yellow eyes. She had been his mistress since he was sixteen. He would miss her, he mused as he crawled under the covers and took her in his arms. But she was fast becoming another complication he could no longer afford.

Chapter 10

Eyes closed, Marri rested her forehead against the cold stone wall of her prison cell, grateful to be free of the chains that had bound her. Never in all her life had she been so miserable. Her back burned like the fires of Cuadra. If one stroke of the lash hurt this much, how had Gryff endured so many more? She groaned softly. Her legs ached. Her arms ached. She was hungry. And thirsty. So thirsty.

She kept hoping she would awake in her own bed and discover the past few days were only a horrible nightmare. Although it hadn't all been horrible. Parts of it had been nice. The parts with Gryff...

She glanced at the cell across the way. Chin resting against his chest, he looked like he was asleep, though how he could sleep standing up, with his arms and legs stretched to their limits was beyond her. It had been hours since he'd said. She missed the comfort of his voice. Now, drowning in the heavy stillness of the dungeon, everything seemed worse, if that was possible.

She twitched as something brushed against her ankle, screamed when something fat and brown scurried over her foot and disappeared through a crack in the wall. A rat! She hated the dirty, disease-bearing creatures!

"Marri, are you all right?"

"There are rodents in here!"

"Is that all?" His faint laughter echoed off the walls.

Marri scowled. How could he laugh at a time like this? They were locked in a dungeon. No one knew where they were. No one would come to their aid. Tears stung her eyes. How could something like this have happened to her? All she had ever wanted was to be allowed to marry and raise a family. She wasn't interested in court intrigue, had no designs on the throne. Now, she yearned for nothing more than to return to Brynn Castle, but even that was no longer possible, not when Artur was determined to see her dead.

Tears trickled down her cheeks and she dashed them away with her fingertips. But the harder she tried not to cry, the faster the tears came.

"Marri, crying won't solve anything."

She sniffed. "I know, but I…I can't help it."

"Dry your eyes. I'll get you out of here."

"How?"

"I don't know. But I will. I promise."

She couldn't imagine how he would accomplish it, but he had escaped this dreadful place before, and she pinned all her hopes on that.

Gryff shifted from one foot to the other in a vain attempt to get comfortable even though he knew it was impossible. Serepta had healed his wounds but his whole body ached from the unnatural position of his arms and legs. His limbs were stretched to the limits of their endurance, his muscles screamed for relief. He licked dry lips, wondering if and when Serepta would allow them nourishment.

He glanced over his shoulder, hoping to catch a glimpse of Marri, but it was too dark to see more than a vague outline. He knew she was afraid and in pain. He didn't know where she came from, but he was certain she had never been mistreated in her entire life. He hadn't missed the fact that her skin was baby soft and unblemished, that her hands were smooth and without calluses, that she was totally ignorant of the ugly side of life.

Maybe she really was a princess.

Maybe her father was out there, searching for her with legions of armed warriors.

And maybe Serepta would kiss him on both cheeks, wish him Godspeed, and send him on his way.

He was dozing when the door creaked open and an old woman limped into view, a covered tray in one hand and a torch in the other. She set the torch in a holder, removed the tray's cover, and slid one plate under the door of his cell and another under Marri's. Picking up the tray, she hobbled out of the dungeon.

Moments later, an ape of a man shuffled into view. He had come earlier and released Marri from her bonds. Entering Gryff's cell, he removed the shackles from his wrists and ankles, but didn't unlock the collar's chain from the iron ring in the floor.

Wordlessly, he stepped back into the corridor, locked the door and shambled back the way he'd come.

Gryff's legs were numb and refused to hold him. Stumbling forward, he sank down on his haunches, his stomach growling as the scent of beef and vegetables tickled his nostrils.

Besides the bowl of soup, there was a loaf of dark brown bread and a cup of tepid water.

He ate quickly, the soup's warmth strengthening him. Only when his hunger had been assuaged did he glance in Marri's direction.

She was sitting on the floor, sipping daintily from the crude wooden bowl. Feeling his gaze, she looked up. "How are you feeling?"

"I'll be all right. How about you?"

"My back hurts." After what he had been through, Marri felt guilty for complaining. Still, the witch had healed Gryff, while the wound in her back was still raw and oozing blood. She could feel the wetness, warm against her skin. It should have stopped bleeding by now. Why hadn't it?

"I'm sorry for getting you into this."

"It's not your fault," she said quietly. "How long do you think she'll keep us down here?"

"Until she tires of us, or until…"

Marri stared at him, all the color draining from her face. "Or until we're dead?"

"Don't think about it. Brooding won't help."

Nodding, she set the bowl aside, her appetite gone. Gryff had promised to get her out of this dreadful place, but she was afraid he was just trying to make her feeling better. She wanted desperately to believe him, but she was sorely afraid that she was never going to see her father or her sister again.

She was still trying to absorb that fact when the door opened and Serepta entered the dungeon. She looked cool and elegant in a long blue gown trimmed in white fur.

With a low groan, Gryff stood.

Lifting her staff, Serepta pointed it at the collar around Gryff's neck. "I would see the wolf."

Gryff shook his head. "No."

"I'm bored," Serepta said. "You can amuse me, or…" Slowly, she swung her staff in Marri's direction. "She can."

Marri glanced from Gryff to Serepta and back again, her eyes widening as Gryff's body transformed. One moment he was a man-- the next, a large black wolf stood in his place. She stared at him, mesmerized by the creature's size.

"Astonishing, is it not?" Serepta mused. "I have seen him do it dozens of times and yet it never fails to amaze me." Unlocking the cell door, she stepped inside. A touch of her staff freed the chain from the iron ring in the floor. Taking hold of the end, she strolled out of the cell.

The wolf padded behind her.

Marri watched the two of them until they were out of sight, her mind reeling at what she had seen.

Serepta left the castle by a side door that led into a walled garden. It was her favorite place, created by her own hand. Wildflowers bloomed here both summer and winter. Lacy ferns shared space with blood-red roses. Trees grew to remarkable heights, their branches intertwining at one end of the garden, providing a leafy canopy that blocked both sun and rain. Footpaths meandered through the foliage; stone benches stood at intervals. Brilliantly colored peacocks wandered the grounds. Statues of soldiers and warriors and maidens stood forever frozen in time. At first glance, they appeared made of stone, but anyone looking closely could see they weren't statues at all, but men and women who had been frozen in time. The truth was in the horror reflected in their eyes.

She paused in front of one of them now. He had been a young

man, vain and foolish, with beautiful blue eyes and a wayward tongue. If he still possessed the power of speech, she had no doubt he would have gone down on his knees and begged for her forgiveness. Pleaded with her to end his torment, but it was too late for that. Eternally too late.

Smiling, she patted his shoulder and moved on. She had filled the garden with statues of people who had displeased her.

The wolf walked beside the witch, seething with impotent rage as she stopped before each poor unfortunate wretch who had been foolish enough to provoke her wrath. He supposed he should be grateful he wasn't one of them. But, statue or slave, he was still under her power, his freedom gone, his only hope of survival to suppress his anger and obey her commands.

He growled low in his throat. He had escaped before. He could do so again, though taking Marri with him would make it more difficult. But he couldn't leave her behind, didn't want to think about what Serepta would do to her.

He padded beside the witch as she made her way from one end of the garden to the other. When she came to a small alcove, she sat down. He stood in front of her, waiting.

"Shall we do tricks, wolf man?" she mused. "Let me see, where shall we start? Sit. Good boy. Lie down. Roll over." She laughed as he obeyed each command. "Such a good boy." She patted him on the head. "Shake hands." She reached into her pocket and withdrew a bit of meat. "Beg." When he did so, she fed him the morsel, then leaned forward and offered him her cheek. "Have you a kiss for me?"

He stared up at her, stared at her long, white throat, and imagined his teeth sinking into soft, warm flesh…

The collar at his throat vibrated. He whined as it grew tighter, tighter. Damn and blast! How did she always know what he was thinking? And how could he have forgotten her uncanny ability to do so?

He stood his ground, stubbornly, stupidly, daring her to do her worst.

She watched him through narrowed eyes and then, in an elegant gesture, she extended her hand toward him. Pain exploded through his body, sharp, needle-like shards that pierced every inch of his flesh until he trembled convulsively.

There was only one way to end the pain and he was loath to do it.

He curled into a ball, hoping she would make it stop, knowing she wouldn't. Not until he abased himself at her feet.

Time lost all meaning. It was foolish to resist and yet he couldn't bring himself to surrender so soon. It was like a horrible game he could never hope to win and yet, each time she punished him, he hoped for the strength to endure the pain until she grew weary of exacting it. Thus far, it had never happened. Tonight would be no different.

Unable to endure more, he crawled toward her on his belly, lifted his head, and licked her hand.

"I will forgive you this time," she said, her voice as hard and cold as the ground beneath his paws. "Next time, I will give the woman to my guards. They would enjoy her, don't you think?"

Hours later, Serepta returned him to the dungeon. When the chain was again affixed to the iron ring in the floor, he looked up at her, a silent plea in his eyes.

"Tired of being the wolf, are you?" she purred. "Very well. Resume your human form."

When he had done so, she left the cell and locked the door. Looking thoughtful, she stared at Marri for several moments and then she looked at Gryff again. "I think perhaps we will go hunting tomorrow," she said with a mysterious smile. "Rest well until then, my handsome one."

Marri waited until Serepta was gone, and then she moved toward the front of the cell, her hands folding around the bars. "What did she mean by that?"

"I'm not sure," he said with a shrug.

But it was a lie. He knew exactly what Serepta had in mind.

Chapter 11

Artur drummed his fingers on the arm of his chair as he listened to Dunnin's report. "No sign of her?" he said, his voice rising. "No sign of her! How is that possible?"

"I found the tavern where she was last seen, but she was gone and so was the owner. A man I spoke to said he'd seen the two of them leaving the area the day before I arrived."

"I don't suppose this man knew their destination?"

"Only that they were headed north."

"North?" Artur frowned. Why would Marri go north? "And what of Dakkar and Trist?"

"Dead, majesty. I found their remains in a ravine a mile from the tavern." Dunnin cleared his throat. "Scavengers had been at the bodies, but I believe they were killed by wolves."

"I'm not interested in what killed them. Why didn't you follow Marri's trail?"

"I did. It led me to a space port on the outskirts of Bosquetown. The barkeep remembered your sister. Called her a fine-looking…" When Artur's eyes narrowed, Dunnin cleared his throat again. "Said she was very beautiful, majesty." Though no one spoke of it in the King's presence, everyone within the castle walls knew of Artur's unholy love for his sister.

"So, this space port is their last known location?"

"Yes, majesty."

Rising, Artur paced the floor in front of the hearth. Days ago, he had been confident his father was at death's door and then the castle physician had called for Old Wyxx. Artur didn't know what magic the old woman had wrought, but two days later, his father was back on his throne, as hale and hearty as ever.

Filled with rage and frustration, Artur stalked to the table beside his chair, picked up his goblet and hurled it into the fireplace. It broke with a satisfying crash, sending sparkling bits of crystal raining down on the fire.

Whirling around, he jabbed his finger in Dunnin's direction. "I don't care how you do it, I don't care who you have to bribe or kill along the way, but find Marri, or don't come back!"

Bowing his head, Dunnin murmured, "Yes, majesty."

Artur grabbed his plate and flung it at the wall. Where was she? His face a mask of rage, he rounded on Dunnin. "Don't just stand there, you fool! Be gone!"

Dunnin was almost to the door when Artur's voice stayed him. "Hold!"

Dunnin turned, his expression wary. "Majesty?"

"North. You said she was going north."

Dunnin nodded.

"Ironntown. Fenton. Bosquetown." His voice rose with excitement. "The Brynn Sea. Tarnn!" He pounded his fist into his palm. "Of course! Why didn't I think of it sooner? She's gone to the convent in Tarnn. To Annis."

CHAPTER 12

Gryff paced the narrow confines of his prison. Eight paces from one end to the other. Back and forth. The familiar sound of the chain dragging on the floor behind him grated on his nerves, but he continued to pace, hour after hour. Back and forth.

From time to time, he glanced at the cell across the way where Marri slept. He envied her the ability to rest in such a place. The last time he had been Serepta's prisoner, he had slept only when exhaustion claimed him. The witch had come for him at odd hours of the day and night, sometimes demanding his services or his attention, sometimes merely desiring his company so she could gloat.

In time, he had come to realize that in spite of all her powers, in spite of the servants who did her bidding, she was a lonely woman, afraid to trust anyone. Cruelty was her master, suspicion her bedfellow.

She had tortured him, whipped him, starved him, finding joy in each heartless act and yet, at the same time, somehow feeling sorry for the pain she gleefully caused him. If he lived to be a hundred, he would never understand the twisted workings of her mind.

"Gryff? Are you all right?"

He glanced across the way to see Marri sitting up, watching him through shadowed eyes. "I thought you were asleep."

"Who could sleep in a place like this?"

He moved as close to the front of his cell as the chain allowed, then hunkered down on his heels, facing her. "You never told me why your brother wants to kill you."

"I don't want to talk about it."

"Still don't trust me?"

"It isn't you. It's this place. It's her."

He nodded that he understood.

"Why does she hate you?"

Gryff blew out a deep breath. "She doesn't hate me. She loves me."

"She has an unusual way of showing it, don't you think?"

"Yeah." But it was true nonetheless. In her own evil, twisted way, Serepta loved him.

"You said she's a vampyre. Why has she never turned you?"

"She doesn't want me to have the kind of power she has." Serepta relished her strength, her preternatural power, and while he would never be as strong or as powerful as was she, even should she make him vampyre, he would be virtually immortal, able to heal his own wounds, able to move with remarkable speed, to vanish from her sight, to raise an army of zombies to fight against her.

"Does she…does she feed off you?"

"No. She tried once, but my blood burned her tongue."

"You don't think she'll feed on me, do you?"

"No. She prefers young men. It's late. You should try to get some rest."

Stretching out on the cold stone floor, he closed his eyes and took his own advice. He would need his strength for the morrow.

Serepta came for him three hours before dawn. Knowing what she wanted, he transformed into the wolf, trotted obediently by her side as they left the keep. Though she was a pitiless hunter in her own right, she enjoyed making him hunt her prey, took pleasure in knowing that killing for her left him wracked with guilt. Once, he would have refused, even though it meant instant punishment. But he couldn't refuse now, not when Serepta had promised to punish Marri in his stead. He had seen what her guards did to the females she gave them.

"There," Serepta said, lifting a graceful hand. "That plump young farmer."

The wolf whined low in his throat. He didn't want to bring the man down, but the farmer's life had been over the moment Serepta decided to have him.

The man let out a startled cry when he saw the big black wolf loping toward him. Dropping the milk pails he had been carrying, the man turned and fled toward the nearest building, but there was no escape.

The wolf was on him before he reached the door.

The farmer stared up at the beast, his eyes wide with horror. Eyes that reflected a moment of hope when Serepta came into view.

The wolf knew what the man was thinking—that the wolf was a pet. That it belonged to the woman. That the woman had come to save his life.

The farmer let out a sigh of relief when Serepta knelt beside him. A smile curved her lips. A smile that revealed sharp white fangs as her eyes went red.

The man was dead before he could scream.

Marri was awake when Serepta returned Gryff to the dungeon. She stayed near the back of her cell, watching in morbid fascination as he resumed his human form, naked save for a scrap of cloth for modesty's sake.

She flinched when the witch looked at her.

Chuckling softly, Serepta left the dungeon.

Marri's gaze moved over Gryff. He sat cross-legged on the floor, his head bowed, his hands clenched, his whole body taut. The witch had taken him hunting. What did that mean, exactly? Something horrible, she thought, to make him look so wretched.

"Gryff?"

"She makes me hunt her prey," he said flatly. "And watch while she kills them."

Marri stared at him, horrified by the images those few words had conjured in her mind.

How many times had the witch made him hunt her prey? How did he live with the guilt? Having seen the cruelty the witch was capable of, Marri could hardly blame him for refusing to obey.

And now Serepta was using her as leverage. "I'm sorry," she murmured.

"It's not your fault."

"But now she's using me to make you do her bidding."

"I was doing it long before you came along. If it wasn't for me, you wouldn't be here."

"I just want to go home," Marri whispered, blinking back her tears.

"Are you ever going to tell me who you are?"

"I will, if we ever get out of here."

He grunted softly. "Fair enough. How's your back?"

"It still hurts."

"Yeah." Closing his eyes, he concentrated on Serepta.

She appeared a moment later. "What do you want?"

"I want you to heal the girl."

Serepta snorted. "Why would I do that?"

"I'll do whatever you want. Just heal her."

Serepta glanced at Marri, and smiled. "You have little choice but to do as I ask," she reminded him.

He didn't respond, merely sat there, waiting.

She looked thoughtful a moment. "Whatever I ask? Willingly?"

Jaw clenched, he nodded.

"Very well."

Turning toward Marri, Serepta muttered an incantation, then opened the door to Gryff's cell. "Come along, my pet. I've waited a long time for this."

"Not so fast. Cay, is the pain gone?"

"Yes."

Nodding, he stood and followed the witch out of the dungeon.

Marri stared after him. What had she done? She never should have told Gryff she was hurting, but how could she have known he would call the witch?

What would Serepta do to him? She had seen the revulsion in his eyes when he agreed to do whatever the witch asked. Marri shuddered. How could she ever repay him for his kindness?

She curled up on the floor, shivering. The only thing that made what she had done bearable was the certainty that Serepta wouldn't kill him.

Knowing sleep was her only escape from this awful reality, she closed her eyes, but sleep wouldn't come. Instead, she found herself thinking about Gryff and Serepta. He had said the witch loved him…had Serepta taken Gryff to her bed?

The thought sent an unexpected shaft of jealousy spearing through her.

And kept her awake far into the night.

Chained to the wall in Serepta's room, the wolf lay on the floor, his head resting on his paws. He had spent the previous four hours fulfilling her every desire. The woman was insatiable. He had often thought she would have made one hell of a lightskirt.

She had ordered him to shift when she finished with him. And now she reclined in an ornate bathtub filled with scented water, a satisfied smirk curling her lips.

He wondered what the odds were that she would let him use the tub when she was finished. At that moment, he wanted nothing more than to scrub her scent from his body.

Or rip her heart from her chest.

Eyes narrowed, she turned to stare at him.

Damn. He knew she could read his thoughts when he was in human form. Could she read the wolf's thoughts, too?

"Change," she said.

Wiping all thought from his mind, he resumed his own form.

"Come wash my back."

Jaw clenched, he did as bidden.

"You could use a bath." Rising, she held out her hand, a silent demand for him to fetch her towel.

After drying off, she pulled on a silk robe. "You stink."

"Whose fault is that?"

She slapped him for his insolence. "Get in the tub."

Resisting the urge to slap her back, he sank into the water. The chain attached to his collar rattled against the side of the tub.

A moment later, one of her maids came in to change the sheets on the bed. Another servant brought him a pair of loose-fitting breeches. The witch must be feeling generous, he thought. She usually kept him naked save for a scrap of cloth to cover his loins.

When the maids left, Serepta knelt beside the tub and washed him, thoroughly, from head to heel. Had it been any other woman, he might have enjoyed it. As it was, it was all he could do to keep from flinching every time she touched him.

When she finished, he stepped out of the tub and into his trousers.

Going up on her tiptoes, she kissed him. "We must do this again. Soon."

He nodded curtly.

"Who's the girl?" she asked.

"I told you before, I don't know anything about her except her name."

"She amuses you?"

He shrugged. "She was a pleasant diversion."

"I think she's more than that."

"Think whatever you like."

"You won't mind if I kill her, then?"

"I'd rather you didn't. It's nice having company in the dungeon."

To his surprise, the witch laughed.

The next thing he knew, he was back in his cell, his chain affixed to the bolt in the floor. Breathing a sigh of relief, he sat down, his back braced against the wall, his gaze on the woman locked in the cell across from his.

Had his words bought her some time?

Or condemned her to death?

Chapter 13

In the morning, shortly after the witch had come for Gryff, a dour-faced guard appeared outside Marri's cell.

She couldn't stop shaking as he led her out of the dungeon, up a narrow, stone staircase, then down another. She feared it led to another dungeon. Or, worse, a place of execution. Instead, it was a kitchen A dozen women clad in long gray dresses and white aprons looked up as the guard pushed her into the room.

"Bellina!"

"Aye?" A short, plump woman with white hair looked up from the pot she was stirring.

"She's in your charge now," he said, giving Marri a shove. "If she escapes, you die." He didn't wait for a reply, merely turned and strode away.

Bellina waddled over to stand in front of Marri. Taking Marri's hands in hers, she touched the backs, studied the palms, and barked a snort of disdain. "Never done a day's work in your life, have ye?"

Marri shook her head.

The woman gestured at a long table. "Get along over there with ye. Old Marna will put you to work making bread until we toughen you up some. Are ye deaf, girl? Get along with ye now!"

Head high, Marri threaded her way to the bread table where she spent the next four hours learning to make bread. As she formed loaf after loaf, she could only wonder how many people resided in the witch's castle.

There was no rest for those who worked in the kitchens. Everywhere she looked, girls and women toiled - not only chopping meat and vegetables to fill the huge pots on the stove, but plucking chickens, washing mountains of pots and dishes, scrubbing the floors.

By the end of the day, Marri's hands ached, her legs were weary, but, by Hathrinn's horns, she knew how to make bread!

Gryff was bone-weary after a day of hunting with Serepta. Covered in dirt and grime, he staggered into his cell, grimacing as the guard secured his chain to the floor. Every day, the collar at his throat felt heavier. Every day, he felt himself sinking deeper into despair. Only Marri's presence made his life bearable...

Marri! Suddenly aware of the silence from the other cell, he sank to his knees. He didn't have to look to know she wasn't there.

He stared at the empty cell, his heart turning cold. Had Serepta done the unthinkable? Guilt pierced his soul. If anything had happened to Marri...He shook his head. He deserved whatever happened to him, but Marri...he doubted if she had ever done a wicked thing in her whole life. All his fault. All his fault...

Steeped in despair, he paid little attention at the sound of footsteps, though, in a distant corner of his mind, he knew a moment of relief that it wasn't Serepta.

"Gryff?"

"Marri!" Relief unlike anything he had ever known washed through him. She was alive.

"I've brought your dinner."

Rising, he moved toward the front of his cell. The guards hadn't shortened the chain, as usual, allowing him to move freely. His gaze moved over her. Her cheeks were flushed, her hair and clothing spattered with flour. But she was alive.

Smiling faintly, she slipped the tray through the opening beneath the bars. "I made the bread."

He didn't miss the note of pride in her voice. It was, he thought, probably the first time she had ever been inside a kitchen.

"I managed to sneak you a few extra slices of beef."

"Thanks."

"You should eat it while it's hot."

Hunkering down on his heels, he pulled the tray toward him. "So, she's got you working in the kitchens?" He slapped a few pieces of meat on the bread and took a bite.

Marri nodded.

He took another bite, then looked up at her and smiled. "Best bread I ever ate."

Her smile went straight to his heart. He wolfed down the rest of it, then stood, needing to be near her.

"I should go."

"Yeah."

But she made no move to leave, sucked in a breath when he reached through the bars, his hand reaching for hers.

Marri gasped as heat seemed to leap from his hand to hers, then spread through her like liquid fire. She stared up at him, eyes wide and scared, like a frightened doe.

His hand slid up her arm, cupped her nape, drew her slowly closer, closer. His gaze trapped hers and she leaned toward him, heart pounding like a wild thing as he lowered his head, his mouth covering hers.

Her eyelids fluttered down, shutting out the world and everything in it except Gryff and the sweet excitement of his lips moving over hers. His arm curled around her waist, making her wish there were no bars between them, that she could feel the length of his body pressed to hers.

She felt bereft when he let her go, bereft and empty and yearning for more.

With a shake of his head, he moved toward the far side of the cell, taking the tray with him. Dropping down on his haunches, he grabbed a handful of meat and stuffed it in his mouth.

Marri stared at him, confused by his abrupt withdrawal, until she heard the creak of the dungeon door.

A moment later, the witch swept into the corridor.

She glared at Marri. "What are you doing here?"

Marri bowed her head. "Bellina ordered me to deliver Gryff's tray. I was just leaving."

Eyes narrowed with suspicion, Serepta looked at Gryff, who was tearing a chunk of bread off the loaf on his tray. Pinching Marri's arm, the witch gave her a push. "Go back to the kitchens where you belong."

With a last, hasty glance at Gryff, Marri fled the dungeon.

"So," he said, wiping his mouth with the back of his hand, "you put her to work."

"Do you object?"

"Hell, no," he said, shrugging one shoulder. "Why should I?"

"Why, indeed?"

Her gaze burned into his. It took all Gryff's control to meet it without flinching. "What do you want?"

"I've arranged a fight for tomorrow night between you and one of Jarrod's hellhounds. Best get a good night's sleep. Your opponent has never been beaten."

Reaching for another slice of meat, he said, "Neither have I."

"I have a lot riding on the outcome. If you lose, the girl dies. Sweet dreams, my pet."

On that happy note, she snuffed the light and left him there, alone in the dark.

Gryff paced the floor. Jarrod was a local warlock who raised hellhounds. The creatures were fearless fighters. Serepta had threatened to pit him against one of them before, but this was no threat. It didn't take much imagination to figure out why she was willing to let him fight one now.

She was punishing him.

Because of Marri.

The witch left him locked in his cell all the next day. No one brought him food or water.

Chained to the floor like a wild animal, there was nothing to do but pace the narrow confines of his prison.

Time dragged on. Just when he thought the day would never end, Serepta appeared at the cell door.

Clad in a gown of royal blue velvet, her hair coiled into a crown, she looked every inch a queen. A wave of her hand opened the door.

Stepping into the cell, she unlocked the chain from the ring in the floor, scooped up the loose end, and led him out of his cell.

He followed like a dog on a leash, his body tensing, adrenaline flowing, as they made their way to the small arena adjacent to the gardens.

Perhaps a hundred screaming, foot-stomping people filled the stands.

Jarrod stood in the middle of the arena, his hellhound on a short leash beside him.

The beast, large and well-muscled, must have weighed close to three hundred pounds.

Serepta nodded at the warlock. "This is not a fight to the death," she said, her voice carrying to the top tier of the arena. "A winner will be declared when one of the opponents concedes defeat." Her gaze rested on Jarrod. "Is that clear?"

Eyes filled with disdain, the warlock grunted. "Afraid your beast will lose, are you?"

Her mouth tightened. "I'm afraid of nothing. I thought only to spare your pet."

"We are undefeated. I have nothing to fear. Do you?"

Knowing what was coming, Gryff swore under his breath. And sure enough, she said the words he dreaded.

"Very well, to the death, then."

The crowd roared its approval.

The hellhound grinned.

At a word from Serepta, the collar fell from his neck and into her hand.

Gryff glared at her as she tucked it into the pocket of her skirt.

"Remember, the girl's life is in your hands. If the wolf runs away, she dies. If you lose, she dies." Serepta lifted one brow. "Do you intend to fight the beast in human form?"

Gryff shook his head. Quietly cursing Serepta for agreeing to a fight to the death, he transformed—not into the black wolf, but into a hellhound the same size as his opponent. He hated to let Serepta know he could transform into something besides the wolf, but there was no way he could defeat Jarrod's hound in wolf form.

A gasp rolled through the arena as he bared his teeth.

Startled, the witch stared at him in disbelief, then vanished from the arena. Serepta appeared in the front row moments later. Staff in hand, she stood behind a wide-eyed Marri, a reminder, no doubt, that if he lost, Marri's life would be forfeit.

Teeth bared, Gryff faced his opponent.

Growling, hackles raised, teeth bared, the hellhound charged.

Gryff met him head-on. It was like hitting a brick wall.

They came together time and again, teeth and claws rending flesh. In minutes, both were bloodied. Gryff's jaws closed on the hellhound's ear, tore it off with a jerk of his head, and spit it out.

With a roar, the hellhound renewed its attack. When they came together again, Gryff's paws slipped on the bloody ground. Before he recovered his footing, the beast's jaws locked on his left foreleg.

The sound of cracking bone brought the crowd to its feet.

Knowing he had to end the fight soon or die, Gryff gained his feet, then stood, his left foreleg useless, his tail tucked between his legs in a gesture of defeat. When the hellhound charged again, he rolled onto his back, waiting for the just the right moment. When it came, he lunged upward, teeth closing on the hellhound's neck. A vicious twist ripped out the hound's throat. The beast stumbled backward, then fell and lay still.

Gryff staggered to his feet, stood there, breathing heavily, blood dripping from numerous wounds, while the crowd stomped and cheered.

A short time later, he was back in his cell, shivering and soaking wet after being hosed down by one of the guards. He had thought fleetingly of shifting into a hawk. With luck, he might have made it to safety before one of her knights shot him down, but he couldn't leave Marri behind to face Serepta's rage.

As though reading his mind, she had entered the arena, replaced his collar. Then, with a murmured incantation, she had healed his leg and handed the chain to one of the guards. Now, he stood passive as one of the guards secured the chain to the floor.

His head jerked up when he heard Serepta's footsteps coming down the corridor.

A moment later, she stood outside his cell, her eyes gleaming with speculation. "Can you transform into any animal you wish?"

He nodded, his expression sullen.

"That's how you escaped before, isn't it? You transformed into a smaller creature? Very clever, my pet. I see that I will have to conjure a new collar, one that will grow larger or smaller as you do."

Dammit!

Serepta laughed softly, inordinately pleased with her cleverness. "The girl will bring your dinner shortly." Shoulders slumped in defeat, Gryff stared after her. Once Serepta fashioned a new collar, he would never get away from her.

Chapter 14

Marri sat on the floor outside Gryff's cell, watching him sleep. She had brought him a tray earlier. He had eaten, then stretched out on the cold stone floor, asleep as soon as he closed his eyes.

She couldn't blame him for being exhausted. After what he'd been through, he was lucky to be alive. Never in all her life had she seen anything so brutal, or been so afraid for another's survival.

Sighing, she rested her forehead against the bars and closed her eyes, her thoughts turning toward home. Was her father well? Was Artur still hunting for her? Had anyone heard from her mother? Was Annis still happy in the convent?

She glanced at her surroundings. Living here, in Serepta's realm, was like stepping into the past. There was no technology here. No tele-screens or communications devices of any kind. Was that by Serepta's choice? Now that she thought about it, she hadn't noticed any Landskiffs or space ports since they left the bigger towns behind.

Suddenly homesick, she thought of Brynn Castle. Though it was ancient, it held all the modern conveniences she so missed - places of entertainment, luxurious bathtubs and showers with hot and cold running water, soft beds covered by thick quilts, kitchens with modern ovens and refrigeration.

A sound from inside the cell drew her attention. Looking up, she saw Gryff thrashing on the floor. "Gryff! Gryff, wake up! You're having a nightmare."

He woke with a start, his eyes wild as he jackknifed into a sitting position. He relaxed visibly when he saw her. Mumbling, "Sorry," he stretched his arms and back, then stood.

Marri rose also. "I should go before Bellina sends someone looking for me."

Gryff nodded.

Her gaze moved over him. Remarkably, his injuries had all healed, though the scars remained. "Are you all right?"

He grunted softly as he moved toward her. "I'm fine." Reaching though the bars, he took her hands in his. In spite of the hours she worked in the kitchen, her skin was still smooth and soft. "How about you? Are you doing okay?"

She stared up at him, unable to speak. At his touch, warmth spread through her, settling deep within her.

"Marri." He whispered her name as his hands slid around her waist, drawing her closer.

Leaning against the bars, she went up on her tiptoes, eager for his kiss. As had happened before, the dungeon, the bars, the ugliness that surrounded her, all fell away. There was only Gryff, his arm around her waist, his free hand stroking up and down her back while his mouth moved over hers, evoking thoughts and sensations she had never known before. Feeling suddenly bold, she slid her hand through a gap in the bars, let her fingertips explore the expanse of his naked chest, the muscles that bulged and flexed in his arm. She wished there were no bars between them, wished she could melt into his embrace and never leave.

She sighed with regret when he lifted his head.

"How brave are you?" he asked.

"Not very." If she had any courage at all, she would have stayed home and confronted Artur instead of running away.

"You want to get out of here, don't you?"

"More than anything. But how?"

"I haven't figured that out yet, but you need make yourself scarce. She's coming."

Marri didn't hesitate. Turning away from the cell, she ran down the corridor as fast as her legs would carry her. She ducked through the first doorway she saw, praying Serepta hadn't seen her.

Gryff was hunkered down in a corner, eyes closed, when Serepta appeared. He didn't have to see her to know she was there. He had heard her footsteps in his nightmares, smelled the faint scent of foxglove that clung to her.

Foot tapping impatiently, she said, "I know you're awake."

Heaving a sigh, Gryff opened his eyes. "What mischief are you planning now?"

"Mischief? Why, none at all. Because of your win today, I've come into possession of something I've always wanted."

"Yeah? I thought you just conjured whatever you wanted."

"In most instances, I do. But there are some things even I haven't been able to conjure. A winged Pegasus is one of them."

"Jarrod wagered a Pegasus? I didn't think they really existed."

Reaching into her pocket, she withdrew a collar. It was similar to the one he already wore, only wider. Probably heavier. "I was able to conjure this."

A wave of her staff opened the cell door.

Gryff backed away from her as far as his chair would allow.

"If you resist, the girl will suffer for it."

He bit back the curse that rose in his throat, stood acquiescent as she removed the old collar with a touch of her hand and put the new one in place, chanted a few words that fused the ends together.

"You will not be able to slip out of this one," she said, smiling. "It will grow or shrink as you do. You can try it out tonight. No matter what you do, you will not be able to trick your way out of it, or dislodge it."

Resisting the urge to touch the new restraint, he said, "You never told me what you wagered," though he was pretty sure he already knew the answer.

"The girl, of course."

The thought of Marri—young and innocent—being mauled by Jarrod made Gryff's stomach clench.

"I don't know who she is," Serepta went on, "but she's more than some mere peasant, of that I'm certain. Tonight, I intend to discover the truth."

'What if she won't talk?"

Serepta's laughter filled the air. "I saw your little love scene. I think, with the right persuasion, she'll tell me everything I want to know."

Fear knotted in Gryff's gut. He knew just what kind of persuasion the witch had in mind.

Marri glanced at her surroundings. Save for the chair she occupied, there was no furniture in the room. No carpets on the floor, no tapestries on the walls. No windows, only a single door. A thick iron bar hung from the ceiling. Brown stains marred the stone floor beneath it.

She jumped when the door opened, felt her heart skip a beat when Gryff stepped into the room. Two burly guards followed close behind him. Wordlessly, they secured his hands to the iron bar, then left the room, closing the door behind them.

Marri stared at Gryff. "What's going on?"

"Serepta's going to ask you a few questions."

"What kind of questions?"

"She wants to know who you are."

Marri's eyes widened.

"Exactly. Faster than you can say ransom, she'll be in touch with your brother."

Her face paled. "And he'll kill me. But, what does that have to do with you?"

Knowing it was useless, he tugged against his bonds. "She thinks you care for me…"

"And that hurting you will make me tell her what she wants to know."

"Exactly. No matter what she does, don't tell her the truth."

"But…"

"She won't kill me. Whatever she dishes out, I can take it." He glanced at the door. "She's coming."

Serepta entered the room, staff in hand. She smiled at Marri as she closed the door. "Well, well, here you are. I assume Gryff has told you why we're here."

Marri nodded.

"So, we can do this the easy way," the witch purred, "or the hard way. The easy way is for you to tell me who you are. The hard way is for you to refuse, although not for you. He'll be the one to suffer."

Marri looked at Gryff.

He stared back at her, his face impassive.

"My name is Cay. I was at Bosquetown on my way to Fennton when your guards kidnapped us."

Serepta sighed dramatically. Then, with a shake of her head, she murmured an incantation.

Marri gasped as Gryff writhed in his bonds, his face contorted in agony, every muscle taut.

"Are you sure you don't want to change your answer?" Serepta asked.

From the corner of her eye, Marri saw Gryff shake his head, almost imperceptibly.

Voice trembling, she repeated her former answer.

A low groan rose from Gryff's throat as tiny cuts opened across his chest, on his arms and legs. Bright red blood leaked from the wounds, dripping into the iron grate at his feet.

"Last chance," Serepta said.

Marri bit down on her lip to keep from crying out as the cuts grew deeper, bled harder, faster, until his chest, arms and legs were covered with crimson. "I'm Marri of House Treymanne. My father is King Leonid of Brynn Tor." She stared at Gryff. Breathing heavily, covered in blood and sweat, he sagged in his bonds, his dark eyes defiant.

"Daughter of a king," Serepta murmured. Eyes narrowed, she poked Gryff with her staff. "How did you come by such a prize?"

"I met her at my place." He drew a deep shuddering breath. "I didn't know who she was."

Serepta lifted a skeptical brow. "What were you doing in Bosquetown? Where were you taking her?"

Marri held her breath as she waited for his answer.

"A couple of thugs broke into my house looking to kill me. I figured you sent them, so I lit out." He took a deep breath. "I couldn't leave her behind so I brought her along. You know," he said with a wicked leer. "For company."

"And you," Serepta said, focusing her gaze on Marri. "What were you doing in Bosquetown?"

"I was traveling to Fennton to…to visit a friend of the family who…who wasn't feeling well."

"Dressed like a peasant?"

"I often go out in disguise."

"Without bodyguards?" Serepta scoffed. "Without any protection at all?"

"We were attacked on the road. My men were killed. I was lucky to get away with my life."

"Well, I'm sure your father will be more than happy to learn you're alive and well. And grateful enough to offer a nice reward, I should think. Mayhap even to the half of his kingdom." Serepta didn't miss the frantic look the girl sent in Gryff's direction, or the way his hands tightened on the bar overhead. Whatever the reason, it was obvious the girl wasn't eager to return home. And just as obvious that Gryff knew it. And now, Serepta thought, so did she. "I'll send word to your father in the morning, princess. Until then, we can't have you languishing in the dungeon, can we? Come along, my dear."

With a last frantic glance at Gryff, Marri followed Serepta out of the room.

Alone, Gryff gave voice to the pain lancing through him in a long, low groan. His body ached, inside and out, from head to foot.

He lost track of how long he hung there, couldn't stand on his own two feet when Serepta's guards came to take him back to his cell. After dumping him inside, they locked the door. Swamped in pain and misery, he closed his eyes and let the darkness carry him away.

Marri hadn't known what to expect when Serepta ushered her up the stairs and down a long, winding corridor lined with doors of different hues, all of which were closed.

The witch paused at the last room on the left. "Make yourself at home," she said, opening the door. "I'll send one of the maids up with towels and a change of clothes."

With a nod, Marri stepped into the room. It was large and square, with a canopy bed, a white dresser, and a rocking chair. A large screen hid a bathtub that filled with hot water while she watched.

Minutes later, one of the kitchen maids entered the room carrying several towels, a robe, and a number of dresses. She smiled uncertainly, obviously wondering what Marri had done to be promoted from maid to pampered guest as she placed the towels on the table and laid the dresses out on the bed.

Marri nodded her thanks.

"Will there be anything else?" the maid asked.

"That will be all, thank you."

Dropping a proper curtsey, the maid left the room, closing the door behind her.

After a moment's indecision, Marri undressed and stepped into the tub. She couldn't help feeling guilty as she sank down into the fragrant water. What right did she have to be surrounded by such luxury when Gryff was hurt, bleeding, all because of her?

But it had been so long since she bathed, and the water felt so good…she consoled herself with the thought that refusing to enjoy the bath wouldn't do anything to ease Gryff's pain. If the situation were reversed, she would want him to enjoy whatever comforts the witch offered while he could. Rationalizing didn't ease her guilt and she washed quickly, then stepped out of the tub.

After drying her hair, she donned the robe. Too nervous to sit, she paced the floor. What would her father do when he learned his daughter was being held prisoner? Would he pay a ransom for her return? Was her father even alive, or, in his haste to secure the throne, had Artur killed their father as he had so callously killed their brothers?

What would her life expectancy be if she returned to Brynn Tor?

Worry as she might for her own life, she couldn't stop thinking about Gryff. Had he been returned to his cell, or had Serepta left him in that dreadful room to bleed to death?

She didn't know how long she'd been pacing when the door opened and the same kitchen maid came in carrying a covered tray. She placed it on the table, scooped up Marri's discarded clothing and left the room.

Marri sat on the bed, her stomach growling as she lifted the cover, revealing a whole roast chicken, half a loaf of bread and several slices of cheese.

Suddenly ravenous, she devoured half the chicken, most of the bread, and two slices of cheese. And then, again feeling guilty, she wrapped the leftovers in her napkin. She sat there a moment, gathering her courage, and then she tiptoed out of the room, hoping Serepta had returned Gryff to his cell. Hoping she could find her way there and back before the witch came looking for her.

Gryff stared at the ceiling, wondering how long he'd been out of it. Groaning, he turned onto his side. It took him a minute to realize that the guards had neglected to refasten the chain to his collar. His hands and feet were free. He grunted softly. If Serepta discovered their negligence, they would undoubtedly pay a heavy price.

Serepta. He sat, cradling his head in his hands. His whole body ached, but he could live with the pain. Right now, he had to think of Marri. He had to get out of here, had to get Marri out of here. Once Serepta had collected whatever reward the king was willing to pay, Serepta would send her home. To her death.

He tensed when he heard someone at the door; a moment later, Marri was standing outside his cell. "Damn, girl, what are you doing here?"

Before she could answer, other footsteps sounded on the stairs. Eyes wide, she ducked out of sight around the corner moments before one of the guards came into view.

"Seems like I forgot something." The man shoved the key into lock, then opened the door.

Gryff kept his expression blank as Marri tiptoed up behind the guard and hit him over the head with a length of wood she must have found in the corridor. He grinned as the guard dropped to the floor, face down. Grabbing the guard's coat, he shrugged it on. "Let's go."

"Go?" Marri frowned at him. "Go where?"

"Just follow me."

He led her away from the main entrance to a trapdoor that opened onto a wooden stairway that descended into a narrow, winding, pitch black corridor. She wrinkled her nose against the stink, clung to his hand as he guided them unerringly through the darkness.

Just when she thought it would go on endlessly, she saw a ray of light. Minutes later, they were standing in what had once been a catch basin for the castle's garderobes.

She followed him up a set of stone steps, then around several buildings, each one further away from the castle, until they reached a tall, iron gate secured with a heavy lock.

"Now what?" she asked, nervously glancing from side to side.

"If luck is with us, we're getting the hell out of here."

"And if it isn't?" she asked, glancing over her shoulder.

"We'll be no worse off than we were before." It all depended on the collar at his neck. Had the witch activated it so he couldn't change shape?

Marri stared at him, her brow creased with worry. Well, he couldn't blame her. A lot was riding on what happened in the next few seconds.

Muttering, "Here we go," he willed himself to change into a giant.

Marri stared at him as he grew taller, broader, until he stood higher than the top of the wall.

Sending her a grin, he tore the gate from the wall and tossed it aside; then, to her further amazement, he transformed into a black stallion with a flowing mane and tail. When the animal went down on its knees, Marri scrambled onto its back.

With a toss of its head, the horse gained its feet. Luck was with them.

Clinging to the horse's mane, Marri let out a whoop of exhilaration as they left the castle far behind.

CHAPTER 15

"Gone?" Serepta's eyes narrowed to mere slits. "What do you mean, he's gone?"

Avoiding the witch's malevolent gaze, the guard knelt on the floor, trembling from head to foot.

"Answer me!"

"I…I forgot to attach the chain to his collar, majesty. As soon as I remembered, I hastened back to the dungeon…" He paused to wipe away the sweat dripping into his eyes. "Someone hit me from behind. When I came to, he was gone."

"Someone. Hit. You."

"Yes, majesty."

"And you know not who that was?" Her voice dripped with venom.

He shook his head, unable to force the words past the fear clogging his throat.

"Could it have been the princess?"

With a wordless cry, the guard prostrated himself on the floor at her feet. "I don't know."

"I know!" She roared the words as she drove the tip of her staff into his back. Flames erupted on contact.

The man screamed as green fire engulfed him, eating him alive until there was nothing left but a bit of ash on the floor.

Awash with fury, Serepta paced the room. Where would they go? Not to Brynn Tor. So where?

Hurrying to her room, she filled a bowl with water, added a few drops of his blood, taken from a small vial, then whispered an incantation as she waved her hand over the black water. She cursed when nothing appeared.

"Where is he?" She shrieked the words, but the water remained black, opaque.

How was it possible for him to block her magic? She should have been able to locate him, yet, once again, she had failed. Was it because he was a shape-shifter? If so, why did that give him the power to shield his whereabouts?

Furious, she grabbed the bowl and hurled the contents against the wall.

Returning to the Great Hall, she summoned her knights.

"Find them," she commanded. "Fail me, and your lives will be forfeit!"

Artur leaned forward, hands braced on his knees as he glared at Dunnin. "She wasn't there? You're certain?"

"Yes, majesty."

"You spoke to Mother Superior?"

"Yes, majesty. She swore to me that Marri has not been there."

"And you believed her?"

Dunnin nodded. "I put a sword to the throat of one of the young nuns and told Mother Superior I would slit the girl's throat unless she told me the truth."

Artur nodded. He had little regard for anyone but himself, but he respected those who took holy vows. It was the only reason Annis still lived.

"Majesty?"

Artur waved a dismissive hand. Where was she?

Chapter 16

Relishing the freedom, the speed and power of his horse-form, Gryff galloped tirelessly across the open desert. He could feel Serepta's location spell pushing at the edges of his being, but, as it had the last time he escaped, his own power negated the spell. Had he been in his human form, he would have laughed aloud at the sheer pleasure of thwarting her. Hopefully, their paths would never cross again.

He ran all that afternoon and into the night, pausing only twice to let Marri rest. She needed nourishment and soon.

Gryff slowed as a village loomed ahead. Veering into the cover of a stand of timber, he went down on one knee. After Marri dismounted, he quickly resumed his human form.

His gaze moved over her. "Are you all right?"

"A little tired, that's all. Why did we stop?" She glanced over her shoulder. "I think we should go on."

"In a bit." Rising, he brushed the dirt from his trousers. "I'm going ahead to have a look around. I won't be long." He brushed a lock of hair behind her ear. "Stay here."

She stared up at him, lips slightly parted. She was so beautiful, her hair like a golden nimbus around her face, her eyes as deep and clear as the rivers of Tarnn.

"Marri." Unable to help himself, he drew her toward him, bent his head, and claimed her lips with his. He hadn't meant to care for her, hadn't wanted to get involved in her life, or involve her in his. Now, he couldn't imagine his future without her. And yet, what chance did they have? He had no security, no home, nothing to offer her except a life on the run…

Lifting his head, he smiled down at her. She was on the run, too. Maybe they had more in common than he thought.

"Stay out of sight," he admonished. "And keep quiet."

Giving her one last kiss, he shifted into a large dog and trotted toward the village.

Marri watched Gryff until he was out of sight. What a strange man he was, able to turn into so many different creatures. What was it like, to shift at will? To be a giant one minute and a horse the next? When he was a hellhound, did he think like one? When he was the wolf, did he hunt for prey? The thought made her shudder with revulsion.

Was Serepta looking for them, even now? Had the witch notified her father? If so, would Artur come looking for her? She shook her head. Artur or Serepta? Not a happy choice.

She paced between two tall trees, aware of time passing, of night falling.

Where was Gryff?

There were a lot of dogs in the village. No one paid any attention to another stray.

Gryff scouted the backyards in the area until he found what he was looking for. Resuming his own shape, he stuffed the pilfered clothing into an old sack he found in one of the yards. When that was done, he wandered through the small marketplace, lifting a couple slices of dried meat which he added to his bag, along with several slices of cheese, two bottles of ale, and a loaf of bread.

Slipping into the shadows, he shifted into a dog again, picked up the sack with his teeth, and trotted back to where he'd left Marri.

He found her sitting under a tree, a worried expression creasing her brow.

He dropped the sack at her feet, then resumed his own form.

Marri frowned at him. "Can I ask you something?"

"Sure?"

"When you change from the wolf to your own form, you're…you know…usually naked. But when you changed from the horse, you were clothed."

He grunted softly. "Force of habit, I guess. The wolf is who I am. I never think about clothes when I change back and forth. I generally become the wolf late at night, come home in the dark, and go to bed. Changing from the horse and the giant…with you there…" He shrugged. "Clothes seemed like a good choice under the circumstances."

"But how do you do it?"

"I guess you could call it shape-shifter magic."

"You have magic?"

He shrugged. "Not much."

She nodded, her expression thoughtful, then gestured at the sack. "What's in there?"

"Food. A change of clothes for you."

Peering into the sack, she found a man's shirt, pants, and a hat. Lifting them out, she looked at him askance. "These are for me?"

"You need a disguise." He used the edge of a rock to pry open the bottles and passed her one, then tore off a chunk of bread and offered it to her, along with a slice of meat and cheese.

She murmured her thanks, her gaze still on the clothing, which looked recently washed. Hopefully, they weren't crawling with fleas! Or lice!

There had been one more item in the bottom of the bag—a hooded robe. When they were ready to leave, Gryff pulled it on. As he'd hoped, it hid the collar around his neck.

And even as he touched the wretched thing, pain exploded through his body. With a harsh cry, he dropped to his knees. Damn and blast. Serepta might not be able to find him, but she could still cause him pain. In spite of what the witch said, he should have tried to find a way to cut the damn thing off when he was in the village.

He writhed on the ground, twitching like a bug on a hot rock, while Marri stood nearby, helpless to do anything but watch.

Gradually, the pain receded, leaving him curled in on himself, feeling weak and breathless.

The last thing he wanted to see was the sympathy reflected in Marri's eyes.

Unleashing a torrent of every curse word he knew, he struggled to his feet. "We're leaving."

"Maybe you should rest a little."

"I'm fine." He didn't wait for an answer. Didn't wait to see if she followed him as he struck out, following a dry riverbed, the rough path screened from the village by dry brush and trees. If they continued northward, sooner or later, they'd pass the Brynn Sea. Tarnn lay in a valley somewhere beyond.

Bone weary, Marri doggedly set one foot in front of the other, silently praying that Gryff would soon stop for the night. They had been walking for hours. Night had fallen long ago, and still he plodded on.

She didn't understand why he was so angry with her, and now, almost out of breath, she didn't care. Sleep. She needed to sleep. Her eyes felt gritty and she closed them a moment, let out a startled cry when her foot hit a deadfall. She stumbled over it and landed hard on her shoulder.

Gryff was beside her in an instant, drawing her into his arms. "Are you all right?"

She nodded, too weary to speak.

"I'm sorry," he said, his voice thick with guilt. She had been nothing but kind to him and how had he repaid her? By making her walk for miles with no rest simply because she'd seen him in pain and it had shamed him. "I've been acting like a fool. Forgive me?"

Marri wanted to touch him, to tell him she understood, even though she didn't, but exhaustion claimed her before she could form the words.

Lifting her into his arms, Gryff held her close for a moment before lowering her gently to the ground. After removing his robe, he covered her with it, then stretched out beside her. He had intended to keep watch through the night, but her warmth, her nearness, lulled him to sleep.

Gryff woke with a start, uncertain of what had roused him. Feigning sleep, he opened his senses. Heavy footsteps. Whispers. A faint scent of perspiration.

They were being stalked. The question was, by who? And why?

The only thing he knew for certain was that they weren't Serepta's henchmen. Outlaws, then? Or just troublemakers on the prowl?

He swore silently, wishing he had a weapon, as they drew closer.

He smiled when he realized there were only two of them. He could handle that many on his own.

Easing away from Marri, still sleeping at his side, he shifted.

Marri woke to the sound of screams. Unable to see anything clearly in the darkness, she reached out for Gryff, only he wasn't there.

Were the screams his? Had the witch found them?

Terror kept her frozen in place. And then she heard the wolf's growl. Another scream. Then only silence. Clutching Gryff's robe in her hands, she whispered his name, let out a scream of her own as a cold nose nudged her arm.

A moment later, Gryff hunkered down beside her. "Are you all right?"

She nodded, weak with relief. "Who were they?"

"Nobody to worry about. Just a couple of thugs."

The smell of death stung her nostrils and she searched the darkness. She couldn't see anything. But they were out there. "They're dead, aren't they?"

"Yeah. Why don't you go back to sleep?"

Sleep, she thought. With two dead men out there in the dark? "Do we have to stay here?"

"Not if you don't want to." Taking Marri by the hand, he led her a good distance away.

Finding a stretch of flat ground, he spread his robe for her.

"Did they injure you?" she asked as she sat down.

"No." He eased down beside her. "It's still hours until dawn. Get some rest. I won't let anything hurt you."

She stretched out on the robe, her cheek pillowed on her hand.

Unable to resist, he lightly stroked her hair, tenderness swelling inside him as her eyelids fluttered down. Moments later, the soft, even sound of her breathing told him she was asleep.

He continued to stroke her hair, thinking his chances of getting her safely to Tarnn weren't looking too good. But she couldn't go home, not with a brother wanting to kill her. Not when Serepta knew where to find her.

Gryff woke with the sun in his face. Sitting up, he scrubbed his hands over his jaw. They were miles from Tarnn. They had no food. No water. He couldn't remember if there were any towns nearby.

Rising, he glanced at the surrounding countryside. Flat, barren. No sign of civilization anywhere.

"Gryff?"

"Morning, princess."

Yawning, she sat up. "Where are we?"

"Beats the hell out of me. That's north," he said, gesturing with his hand. "So that's where we want to go."

Nodding, she gained her feet and handed him the robe. She blushed when her stomach growled in a very loud, very unladylike way.

"I don't think there's a town nearby." Folding the robe, he handed it back to her. "We need to make better time, so I'm gonna shift. You ready?"

"I am if you are." She watched, amazed, as Gryff shifted into the big black horse again.

As he had before, he went down on one knee; as she had before, she grabbed a handful of mane and pulled herself onto his back.

In spite of being hungry and thirsty, racing across the desert was exhilarating. She loved the feel of the cool morning wind in her face, the sense of freedom, the sound of the horse's hooves pounding over the barren ground.

Gradually, the desert gave way to patches of green. Cactus and shriveled shrubs grew scarce, replaced by trees that grew taller and more numerous as they continued northward.

Marri had lost track of time when the first house appeared, although it wasn't really a house, but more like a thatched hut. Several others were strung out beyond, growing closer together, larger, nicer, built of wood and brick with tile roofs.

The stallion stopped when they reached the outskirts of a small town. When he went to his knees, she slid off his back. A moment later, Gryff stood before her.

"Is this Tarnn?" she asked, glancing around.

"No. It's too small. And there's no convent." Taking the robe from her, he pulled it over his head. "Stay here. I'm going to go look around."

He sensed it as soon as he neared the fountain in the center of the village square - the unmistakable whiff of magic.

CHAPTER 17

Gryff paused behind the fountain, all his senses going on high alert as the faint signature of witchcraft washed over him. Had Serepta found them already? His gaze swept the village, his tension gradually waning with the realization that it wasn't Serepta's magic he was sensing, nor was it dark magic. Unless he was mistaken, he was picking up on the presence of a powerful witch nearby.

He lifted a hand to the collar at his throat. A witch had conjured it. Perhaps another witch could undo the spell. Maybe even figure out a way to remove the damn thing.

Several people clad in peasant clothing sent glances in his direction. Most were merely curious, a few were wary.

"Sir?"

Sir? Turning, Gryff came face-to-face with a young woman. Short and slim, she was covered head to foot in a robe similar to the one he wore. "Something you want?" he asked.

Hands clasped, she regarded him through mild gray eyes. "I think there is something *you* want."

"Yeah? Like what?"

"Nourishment for yourself and your companion. A change of clothes." She wrinkled her nose. "A bath."

"Who the hell are you?"

"One who can help you, if you'll let me."

"And why would you do that?"

Inclining her head, she murmured, "Perhaps I was mistaken. Forgive my intrusion."

Gryff laid hold on her arm when she started to turn away. "You're not mistaken."

"I live in the house with the blue door. You and your companion are welcome to share my table."

"Obliged."

He watched her walk away, noting that she was soon surrounded by a number of children, all reaching out to touch her.

With a shake of his head, he went to fetch Marri.

"Are you sure we can trust her?" Marri clung to Gryff's hand as the village came into view.

Gryff shrugged. "We'll soon find out."

As they approached the village, Marri noted several open-air stalls located around a pretty bubbling fountain. Vendors sold a variety of goods. A dozen or so houses made a wider circle beyond the stalls. She heard the ring of a blacksmith's hammer, the wail of a baby, the chiming of a distant bell. A church somewhere in the distance, perhaps?

"Where are we going?" she asked as they passed the vendors and made their way down a narrow, dirt road.

Gryff jerked his chin toward a small house with a blue door. "A witch lives there."

Marri came to an abrupt halt. "Another witch!"

"She's a good witch. I think."

"You think?"

"Come on," he said, tugging on her hand. "She offered us food and shelter and we need both."

Marri shook her head. "Why would a stranger offer to help us?"

"I don't know. But I didn't sense anything evil about her, and I'm tired and hungry."

Marri was about to argue further, but her stomach chose that moment to make another unladylike complaint. Hoping they weren't making a terrible mistake, she followed Gryff along the path to the house with the blue door.

The witch opened it before he knocked. "Please, come in," she invited.

As soon as Marri saw the woman, all her misgivings faded away. There was something in the witch's dove-gray eyes that inspired confidence, something in the gentleness of her voice that garnered trust.

"Sit and be comfortable while I prepare you something to eat," the witch said.

"Can I help?" Marri asked.

"If you wish."

Marri glanced at Gryff then followed the witch into the kitchen.

Gryff sank down on the divan, tapped his fingers on the arm while he glanced around a room decorated in earth tones of beige, brown and sage. The furnishings were simple but exquisite—the couch on which he sat, a low table, the plush carpet on the floor, and, in the far corner, a shrine of some kind.

He was almost asleep when Marri plucked at his sleeve. "Our meal is ready."

Rising, Gryff followed her into the kitchen, his mouth watering at the pleasant aromas that filled the air.

The witch indicated a place at the table. "Please, sit."

"Smells good," he remarked, taking the seat she indicated.

The witch nodded her thanks.

Marri sat across from Gryff.

"I am Seleena," the witch said as she filled their glasses with wine.

Gryff introduced himself, then said, "This is Marri."

"King Leonid's daughter. I am pleased to meet you."

"You know me?" Marri exclaimed. "How is that possible?"

"I know many things."

"Do you know where we're going?" Gryff asked.

"To Tarnn."

He frowned. "And where we've been?"

"In Serepta's realm."

"How the hell do you know that?"

"You will not use such language in my presence. I let it pass once. I will not do so again."

Gryff's jaw tightened at the reproof. After taking a deep breath, he murmured, "My apologies. But how do you know that?"

Seleena inclined her head. "I have been blessed with many gifts.

One of them is to read those who come into my presence. I know Marri is seeking refuge in the cloister at Tarnn and that you seek to escape Serepta's power over you. If you wish, I can remove the collar."

"I don't think it can be removed, except by the witch who bespelled it."

Seleena smiled indulgently. "I can undo this one. I am Serepta's mother."

Gryff blinked at her. His first reaction was disbelief. And then distrust. What if the mother was worse than the daughter? Calling on his wolf senses, he took a deep breath, but he detected no evil in the woman or in her home.

The witch regarded him calmly, obviously aware of his scrutiny.

They looked enough alike to be sisters, he thought, but her mother? And then he grunted softly. Witches didn't age the way regular mortals did; and when they did start to show signs of growing older, they often invoked a spell to veil their years.

"The collar," Seleena said as he settled back in his chair. "Do you wish me to remove it?"

"I'd appreciate it."

"I must warn you, it will likely cause some discomfort."

Gryff lifted a hand to the golden collar hidden by his robe. "I'm no stranger to pain. Just get the blasted thing off me."

"Let us finish our meal first."

Gryff nodded. Was it possible she could remove the damn thing? He didn't care how much it hurt to get rid of it. He just wanted it gone.

They finished the meal in silence. A wave of the witch's hand cleared the table.

"If you're ready, I'll remove that collar now," she remarked.

"More than ready." Rising, he pulled the robe over his head and tossed it aside.

When he resumed his seat, the witch moved behind him, her hands resting on his shoulders, gently massaging away the tension. "Relax.   She   cannot   find   you   here."
Gryff closed his eyes as the witch's hands soothed him.

Moments later, she began to sing. He couldn't understand the words, but they wound around him, weaving a spell as her voice grew louder. He tensed as Seleena's hands moved to the collar. He broke out in a cold sweat as her power overwhelmed Serepta's, tearing apart the other witch's spell, wresting it not only from the metal around his neck but seemingly draining it from his very core.

It was a pain to rival the worst Serepta had ever inflicted on him.

A harsh cry escaped his lips as the collar bit into his flesh, as if it was fighting the witch's efforts to remove it, and then, to his amazement, it disintegrated and disappeared.

Gryff blew out a sigh of relief, then glanced over his shoulder. "If there's anything I can do for you...."

"My daughter? How is she?"

"As mean and vindictive as ever."

"She wasn't always so," Seleena remarked. "It was the vampire blood that changed her." She shook her head, as if to clear it. "You are welcome to stay the night, if you wish, though I only have one extra room."

"That'll be fine," Gryff said. "Again, I'm in your debt."

"I'm very tired," Marri said. "Would it be all right if I retire now?"

"Of course. Come, I'll show you to your room. There's a bath waiting. Clean towels. A change of clothing for you both."

Marri looked at Gryff. "Are you coming?"

"No. I'll be along in a while."

She nodded. Eager to be out of her stolen clothing, Marri quickly followed the witch out of the room.

Gryff paced the floor for a few minutes, then, feeling suddenly restless, he left the house.

With the setting of the sun, most of the villagers had retired to their homes. The food stalls were closed. A couple of dogs nosed around the empty stalls.

Feeling free for the first time in weeks, Gryff strolled the empty road. More than once, his hand went to his neck just to make sure the hated collar was really gone.

Seleena was Serepta's mother. Talk about a small world, he thought, and then came to an abrupt halt. Was he being a fool, to trust the mother? Was her offer of shelter merely a ruse to keep them here until Serepta's arrival?

Shit!

For all he knew, the mother could be worse than the daughter!

Suddenly fearing for Marri's safety, he sprinted back to Seleena's house.

CHAPTER 18

Marri reclined in the tub, enjoying the froth of scented bubbles, the luxury of clean hot water. It was wonderful to relax, to have a full belly, to feel safe.

The room, though small when compared to her room at Brynn, was quite lovely, from the colorful quilt on the double bed to the painting on the wall.

She glanced at the door, wondering where Gryff had gone, when he would return. She liked him far too much, spent too many hours dreaming of things that could never be. He was a commoner, unlearned, more than a little rough around the edges. Not that it mattered. Once she entered the convent, she would never see him again.

She wished she could get word to Annis that she was coming, but she dared not try to send a message for fear it would fall into the wrong hands. She wondered briefly if Artur would believe her if she sent him a letter assuring him that she had no designs on the throne. Even if he believed her and welcomed her home, she could never have a life with Gryff. As Princess of House Treymanne, she would be forced to marry a peer of the realm, perhaps to assure peace with another part of the kingdom, or add wealth to Brynn Tor's coffers.

She ran her fingers through the bubbles. Even though she had been in the tub for some time, the water was still hot, the bubbles still abundant. Witchcraft, she mused with a grin. It wasn't all bad.

Marri drifted on the edge of sleep when the bathroom door banged open. She bolted upright, water splashing over the edge of the tub, her heart pounding. Had Serepta found them? She pressed a hand to her heart when she saw Gryff standing in the doorway.

"Are you all right?" he asked, his gaze darting around the room.

"I was until you frightened me half to death. What's wrong?"

"Nothing. Just over-reacting, I guess." He leaned back against the door jamb. Maybe his fears for their safety were groundless.

And then he noticed—really noticed—Marri for the first time. She had piled her hair atop her head, save for a few damp tendrils that framed her face. Bubbles covered her almost to her chin, but Gryff had no trouble picturing the delectable body hidden beneath the soapy water. In a heartbeat, he forgot all about the witch. A fact that was blatantly evident if Marri chose to notice.

She blushed hotly under his lusty gaze. They had spent weeks together. Spent nights within inches of each other. She had comforted him while he cried, seem him in pain. Naked.

That thought made her cheeks burn even hotter.

"Marri."

She blinked up at him, her whole body yearning toward him. Her breath caught in her throat when he took a step toward her, his eyes hot. Surely he didn't mean to ravish her? And hard on the heels of that thought, she found herself wondering if that would be so bad.

Gryff took another step. Another. And then paused. What the hell was he doing? Was he seriously thinking of seducing Marri, Princess of Brynn Tor? Even if he didn't have a price on his head, even if Serepta didn't have her henchmen searching for him, even if he had the means to support a wife, Marri could never be his.

He might be a wanted man and a rogue, but he hadn't yet stooped to deflowering virgins, no matter how tempted he might be.

Cursing under his breath, he pivoted on his heel, stalked out of the room, and slammed the door.

Marri stared after him, blinking back tears of disappointment. She wasn't a complete fool. She knew there was no chance of a future with Gryff, didn't know if he would even be interested if it was possible, but in her heart she had hoped he might take her by force, thereby allowing her to be intimate with a man she cared for while absolving her of guilt.

The thought shamed her. Decent women saved themselves for marriage. But she would never be allowed to marry a man she loved. Shouldn't it be her right to give her virginity to a man she cared for? It was a gift that could be given only once. And she wanted Gryff to have it.

Sighing, she stepped out of the bathtub and reached for a towel, wondering if she had the courage to offer Gryff what he had been reluctant to take.

Marri drew the covers over her shoulders. Hours had passed since she bathed and still Gryff hadn't come to bed. Where was he? Had he shifted and gone running through the night? Or had he decided he would rather sleep on the couch than share a bed with her? She had been so certain it was desire she had seen in his eyes earlier. Had she been mistaken?

She shook her head. He had held her, kissed her. He might not love her, but he wanted her. She was sure of it. And she wanted him.

Sighing, she turned onto her side and closed her eyes.

But sleep wouldn't come.

She didn't know how much time had passed when she heard the soft creak of the bedroom door opening. Her heart skipped a beat when she saw Gryff slip into the room. Though it was hard to see in the dark, she heard the whisper of cloth over skin as he removed his shirt, the soft thud of his boots as they hit the floor.

She held her breath as he walked to the far side of the bed, felt her whole being tense as she waited for him to slide under the covers beside her.

Frowned when he didn't.

Experienced a keen sense of frustration when she realized he intended to sleep on the floor.

Gryff stretched out on the rug, his arms folded under his head and stared up at the ceiling. He could hear Marri tossing and turning, couldn't help wondering if the same itch was keeping them both awake.

Reminding himself that there was no future for the two of them, he put the thought out of his mind. Earlier, while Marri bathed, he had talked to Seleena. She hadn't divulged the reasons for the hard feelings between her and her daughter, but he got the impression that whatever caused the rift had been pretty bad.

All thoughts of witches fled his mind when Marri cried out.

He was on his feet and at her side in a heartbeat.

"Marri." He called her name softly. When she didn't respond, he gently shook her shoulder, jerked out of reach when she began to thrash on the bed.

"No! No! Let me go!"

Grasping her shoulders, he shook her again, harder this time. "Marri, wake up. You're safe."

Her eyes flew open and she stared up at him. "Gryff?"

Sitting on the edge of the mattress, he stroked her cheek. "You were having a nightmare. Go back to sleep."

She shook her head. "No."

"That bad, huh?"

"I dreamed my brother found me. He was going to throw me out of the tower window, like he did that poor kitten."

"He threw a cat out of a window?"

Marri nodded. "It wasn't some horrible boyish prank, either. He was almost twenty-one at the time."

"Sounds like the perfect match for Serepta," Gryff muttered.

Sitting up, Marri wrapped her arms around her middle.

"You're shivering," Gryff said. "Are you cold?"

"No. Would you hold me?"

He didn't answer, simply curled his arm around her waist and drew her close. He swore softly when she rested her head on his shoulder and snuggled against him. Damn. Did she know what she was doing to him? What he wanted to do to her?

Five minutes became ten. Fifteen.

His nerves were strung tight, his whole body throbbing with need, when the soft, even sound of her breathing told him she had fallen asleep.

Easing her down under the covers, he didn't know whether to curse Fate or thank his lucky stars.

Seleena sat in her rocking chair in front of the hearth, one hand stroking the cat curled in her lap. The man, Gryff, had been Serepta's prisoner. As soon as he had entered her house, she had felt the pain her daughter had inflicted on him. Even after all this time, it was hard to believe that her daughter, her only child, had turned into such a monster. How long ago it seemed since she had been not only Serepta's mother, but her mentor and best friend, as well.

She had taught Serepta everything she knew, felt a mother's pride in watching her daughter learn and grow in the art of witchcraft. Serepta had been a gentle child, loving, kind to all—animals, people, the earth. Witchcraft had come easily to her, but that was to be expected. Though Serepta had never known her father, he was the greatest wizard in the land. By the time she was ten, Serepta had mastered fire and water. By the time she was twenty, she had learned everything Seleena could teach her.

And it hadn't been enough. Serepta had wanted more power. And she had found it in the blood of a vampire.

But Seleena's magic—pure and undefiled—remained the stronger of the two.

To prove it, she had cast a protection spell around the couple sleeping in her guest room. It would effectively prevent Serepta from locating the pair when they left here.

She smiled inwardly. All magic carried the signature of the one who conjured it. Her only regret was that she wouldn't be there to see the expression on her daughter's face when she realized who had thwarted her.

In the morning, Marri didn't think she could face Gryff. What must he think of her? Acting like a child, begging to be held because of a nightmare. And then snuggling up against him like some…some…heat flooded her cheeks. Some wanton.

But what else could he think? She had let him kiss her several times when she should have pushed him away. Just thinking about his kisses filled her with a different kind of heat, one that spread through her and settled in the deepest part of her.

Maybe she was a wanton, she thought. Because she surely wanted him.

She glanced around the room, wondering where he was, practically jumped out of her skin when he appeared beside her. "Did you spend the night on the floor?" she asked, pressing a hand to her thundering heart.

He looked at her, then the bed. "Where else?"

Her gaze flew to his naked chest as he uncoiled from the floor in one lithe movement. Shirtless, his hair tousled, a growth of whiskers shading his jaw, he looked roguish and dangerous and more desirable than ever.

Her breath caught in her throat when his gaze met hers. She swallowed hard. "Are we leaving today?"

He nodded. "Reckon so."

Would he make love to her if she asked? When they reached Tarnn, she would plead with the sisters to accept her into their order. Once she had taken her vows, she would never see another man except for the priest who came monthly to hear the nuns' confessions. If he didn't make love to her, no one ever would.

Before she could summon her nerve, Seleena called them in to breakfast. Perhaps it was just as well. As tempting as Gryff was, she knew making love to him wasn't a good idea. And what if she got pregnant? That thought alone changed her mind.

Seleena proved to be a remarkable cook. Good meals had been scarce and Marri thanked her profusely.

Seleena dismissed her thanks away with a wave of her hand. "I enjoy cooking. It isn't often I entertain guests. You should be safe from my daughter until you reach your destination."

"Why's that?" Gryff asked.

"I've woven a spell to prevent her from locating you. But be cautious. She can be treacherous."

He grunted softly. He was well aware of the way Serepta's mind worked. He had the scars—physically and mentally—to prove it.

Seleena refused Marri's offer to help clean up after breakfast. "I know you must be in a hurry to be on your way."

She presented each of them with a change of clothing and when they were ready to leave, she handed Gryff a large sack filled with food and a flagon of wine for their journey.

At the door, Gryff hefted the bag over his shoulder. "Thanks for putting us up and everything."

"I am sorry for whatever pain and suffering my daughter caused the two of you."

"Not your fault. You ready, Marri?"

"Yes. Thank you, Seleena."

Marri followed Gryff out of the house and down the road. She felt the witch's gaze following them until they were out of sight.

Chapter 19

"Do you think we can trust her?" Marri asked as they left the witch's house behind.

"I hope so," Gryff muttered, but he had other things on his mind, like stealing a new ride. They had just about reached the end of the village boundary when he spied a Landskiff similar to the one he'd stolen before, only newer and in much better condition. He glanced around, wondering where the owner was. They hadn't seen any other vehicles in the village.

A glance in the front window showed there was no one in the cockpit, no one idling near the craft.

Striding confidently toward the rear of the skiff, he knocked on the door of the cabin. When there was no answer, he lifted the latch and peered inside. After ascertaining it was empty, he dropped the bag Serepta had given them on the floor and closed the hatch.

Moving with purpose, he guided Marri to the passenger side, opened the door, and lifted Marri onto the seat.

"What are you doing?" she asked.

"Getting us a new ride. Hop in."

When she started to argue, he closed the door, then strolled around to the driver's side and climbed behind the consol. Raising the control panel, he fiddled with the computer, grinned when the skiff's engine roared to life. "Hang on," he warned.

Marri grabbed the door handle, her guilt momentarily swallowed up as the skiff shot forward. It went faster, rode smoother, than the last one. She slid a glance at Gryff, who was grinning like a child with a new toy. When he looked at her, she felt it clear to her toes, found herself grinning back at him. And then she frowned. She had never stolen anything in her life, and now she was an accomplice to a crime. But she didn't care, nor could she ignore the little thrill that ran through her when Gryff winked at her. No one had ever told her that breaking the law could be fun!

Gryff put the Landskiff on Auto-pilot, then sat back in his seat. "We should reach Tarnn tomorrow night," he remarked.

"Really?" Marri stared at him, her heart pounding with excitement. One more day until they reached Aisley Cloister and her sister.

He nodded. "We're making good time. This bucket's a lot faster than the last one." Suddenly restless, he took over the controls again. No doubt she would be glad to see the last of him. She would certainly be safer behind convent walls than with him. Damn and blast, though, he would miss having her around.

Marri sat in her bunk, staring out the window of the skiff. The day had passed quickly. All too quickly, she thought, when she realized that, after tomorrow night, she would never see Gryff again. She blinked back tears, suddenly overcome with a sense of impending loss. The thought of his leaving hurt more than she had thought possible. He was uncouth by court standards. He fought like a savage. He had not a drop of royal blood…but his kisses…She pressed her fingertips to her lips, remembering the touch and the taste of him, knew she would miss him for the rest of her life.

She wiped the tears from her eyes, all thoughts of the morrow forgotten when she saw movement through the window.

Peering through the glass, she saw a big black wolf standing beneath a tree. Was it Gryff? Even as the thought formed in her mind, the animal changed. One minute, a wolf stood there; the next, it was Gryff.

She met his gaze through the window. He made no move to cover his nakedness as he stared back at her. But then, why would he? She had seen it all before.

Her pulse quickened as he strode toward the hatch. A moment later, he stepped inside, fully clothed.

Her disappointment brought a rush of heat to her cheeks.

"Better get some sleep," he said quietly. "We're leaving at first light."

Marri turned onto her side, then onto her back. Sleep. No matter how she chased it, she couldn't catch it. All she could think about was never seeing Gryff again. There was no denying the attraction she felt for him, but now, she realized it was more than that. She liked him. A lot. His subtle humor. His willingness to defend her. If not for Gryff, she would likely be dead now, killed by Trist and Dakkar weeks ago.

The light of the planet's twin moons shone into the cabin. Turning her back to it, she found herself looking into Gryff's eyes—eyes dark with desire.

He wanted her. She felt the pull between them like a tangible force. Thoughts of right and wrong didn't seem to matter when he was looking at her like that, when the outside world seemed to fade away and only they remained.

"You'd better stop looking at me like that," he growled, "or I won't be responsible for what happens next."

Marri stared at him, her breath trapped in her throat. If only he hadn't put it to her like that, leaving the decision—and the guilt, should she say yes—in her hands. "Oh, that's so unfair!"

He frowned at her. "Unfair?"

"I want you so much and I know it's wrong. How can I expect the sisters to accept me when I'm such a wanton? If you'd just…just…" She shook her head when she realized what she was saying. "Never mind."

Sitting up, Gryff raked his fingers through his hair. "I know what you want. You want me to take you without your consent so you don't have to feel guilty about it later."

Marri looked away, her cheeks flaming with shame and embarrassment. It was unfair of her to expect him to take all the blame for whatever happened between them. Murmuring, "I'm sorry," she turned her face to the wall.

She heard him swear softly and then he was sitting on the bunk beside her, one hand lightly stroking her back. "Listen, Marri. There's no use pretending. Like you said, you want me. I want you. Maybe, if you weren't untouched, I'd take you in my arms and make love to you all night long. But I've never deflowered a virgin and I'm not going to start with you. You deserve a hell of a lot more than I can ever hope to give you."

"I think I'm in love with you."

He swore again when he heard the tears in her softly spoken words.

"Marri. You're so young. I doubt you've known very many men. Don't confuse lust for love."

"I know the difference!"

"Do you?" He lifted her into a sitting position, brushed her tears away with the pads of his thumbs. And then, unable to resist, he pulled her into his embrace and kissed her, his mouth devouring hers, his hand skating up and down her back, skimming the curve of her breast. When she was limp and breathless in his arms, he drew away. "Was that love?" he asked. "Or lust?"

She stared up at him, her eyes brimming with tears. "Don't be mean to me, Gryff. This is our last night together."

He knew that, but hearing her say it made it more real, more painful. He'd been in lust a dozen times, but love? Damn and blast. Maybe he was the one who didn't know the difference.

Murmuring, "Forgive me, sweetheart," he drew her into his embrace once again, his hand delving into the wealth of her hair. He wanted her more than his next breath, more than life itself, but like he'd told her, he'd ever defiled a virgin. How could he start now, with the woman who rested so trustingly in his arms? He knew what she wanted. Hell, he wanted the same thing. But she was a princess. Perhaps one day she would be a queen. Surrendering to his desire for her could easily ruin her life. And what if there was a child? No method of birth control was fool proof, and even if it was, he didn't have any.

The chance of a child of his falling into Serepta's hands cooled his ardor.

Easing away from Marri, he kissed the top of her head. "You should get some rest."

She slipped under the covers. When Gryff moved toward his own bunk, she grabbed his hand. "Stay with me?"

He hesitated a moment before stretching out beside her, careful to keep the blankets between them. It didn't help. His body reacted as expected as she pillowed her head on his shoulder. It was, he thought ruefully, going to be a long, painful night.

"Gryff?"

"Yeah?"

"I'm curious about something?"

"What's that?"

"I've never known a shape-shifter before. Are there others like you?"

"I've never met any."

"What did you mean the other night, when you said the wolf is what you are?"

"It's part of me. Changing into anything else requires a lot of effort and concentration. But, like I said, the wolf is who I am." He paused a moment before asking, "Does it bother you?"

"No. On the contrary, I rather like it."

She was one in a million, he thought, and wondered how he would ever let her go.

Chapter 20

Artur sat back, his hands stroking the carved arms of his father's throne—the throne that would soon be his. But at the moment, his attention was on the woman who had requested a private audience with him. She was stunningly beautiful, with waist-length hair and slanted eyes as black as onyx. An air of power clung to her.

Steepling his fingers, he asked, "How may I help you, my lady?"

"I have news of your sister."

"Marri?" He leaned forward. "Is she well?"

"First, a favor."

"Name it."

"She is traveling with a man. I believe they are on their way here."

"Who is this man in league with my sister?"

"He is of little consequence, milord. But he is mine."

"Then what is he doing with my sister?"

"You misunderstand. He *belongs* to me. I am willing to pay you well for his safe return."

Artur regarded her for a moment, then nodded. "Very well. Should he come here, I will hold him for you."

Serepta smiled inwardly. She had attempted to conjure a locator spell to find Gryff and the woman, but it had failed. And she had her mother to thank for it. But it didn't matter. The locator spell would have allowed her to find Gryff sooner, nothing more. Gryff was on the run. There was no place for him to go, and to her knowledge, nowhere for the woman to go but home. Gryff wouldn't let her make the trip alone.

Serepta nodded. For all she knew, Gryff had always intended to return the woman to her brother and claim a reward. Whatever his intention, she would collect him and he would be in her power again. Whether he arrived in days or weeks was of no consequence. Her mother had taught her the value of patience. Sooner or later, Gryff would be hers again.

This time for good.

In the meantime, she would make herself at home in Brynn Tor.

CHAPTER 21

Marri woke slowly, reluctant to leave her dreams behind. In them, Gryff had made love to her, sometimes quickly, sometimes slow and tender, as if she was made of fine crystal. But, fast or slow, it mattered not because she had been in his arms, lost in a magical world that could never be more than a dream.

His arms...she opened her eyes to find that she really was in his arms.

"Morning, princess."

Her gaze slid away from his as, remembering her dreams, she felt a flush climb up the back of her neck.

"You all right?"

She nodded.

"We should be on our way."

"Yes, but...couldn't we wait a few days?"

"You're the one who's in a hellfire hurry to get to Tarnn."

"I know but..." She bit down on her lower lip.

Lifting his hand, Gryff traced the curve of her cheek. "I don't want to leave you, either."

Frowning, he weighed the danger. As far as he knew, no one was hot on their heels. Seleena had conjured a spell to prevent Serepta from locating their whereabouts. The food she had packed them would last for a couple of days if they ate sparingly.

"Two days," he said. "No more."

Marri glanced at Gryff as he climbed into the cockpit, smiled as she admired his profile. He had a fine straight nose, a strong jaw, sculpted lips…she blushed as she wished her dream the night before had been reality. Had he grown more handsome since they met, or was it just that she fell a little more in love with him with every passing day? For love him she did, whether he believed it or not.

Feeling her gaze, he smiled at her.

She felt it all the way to her toes.

Turning his attention back to the road, he checked the nav system, made a hard right and then a left. Thirty minutes later, he brought the skiff to a stop in the middle of a glade surrounded by a pine tree forest.

Marri looked out the window. Tall trees surrounded them. Beyond the trees, a lake sparkled in a splash of sunlight. Lush, rolling hills rose beyond the lake, a refreshing change after days of barren desert. "Where are we?"

"The outer boundary of Tarnn. The convent's about thirty miles east." Stepping out of the craft, Gryff rounded the front and opened her door. "Come on."

"It's beautiful here," Marri said, taking his hand. "It reminds me of a story my mother used to tell me, about an enchanted land inhabited by fairies and elves." She looked up at him, a twinkle in her eye. "Can you transform into an elf?"

"No," he said. And then he laughed "A troll, maybe, or perhaps an ogre."

"No need. I have my brother for that."

Hand in hand, they walked down a gentle slope to the lake. As they drew closer, she saw that it was ringed with flowers in rainbow colors. Tall ferns slow-danced in the faint breeze. She wouldn't have been surprised to see a water sprite or two flitting about.

Gryff paused in the shade of an overhanging branch and drew her down on the velvet grass. Overhead, a gray squirrel with a long fluffy tail chattered at them.

"I don't think he likes us," Marri said.

"I could trap him and roast him for dinner."

"No!" She looked at him in horror.

"Calm down, love, I was joking."

"I don't think you were."

He shrugged. "I've eaten my share of rabbits and squirrels in my day, when there was nothing else." He grinned at her. "Mighty tasty with a little salt and pepper."

"I think he understood you," Marri remarked as the squirrel jumped to another tree and disappeared from sight.

"Maybe. Or maybe he sensed the wolf in me."

Marri looked at him, eyes wide. "Are you serious?"

"Yeah. Some animals shy away from me, though not the predators."

"Are you going to prey on me, Gryff?"

"Marri…." Damn and blast, the woman tempted him almost beyond reason. If she kept looking at him like that….

Muttering an oath, he swung her into his arms and carried her into the lake.

She shrieked as he sank down into the water. "It's like ice in here!"

"You'll get used to it."

When he released her, she let out another cry, then threw her arms around his neck and clung to him like a nettle.

"Come on," he chided, "it's not that cold."

"I can't swim!"

He immediately scooped her into his arms. "Sorry, love." Returning to shallow water, he set her on her feet. "I just thought we could use a little cooling off."

"Next time just say no," she muttered, and headed for shore.

Gryff stared after her, wondering how much longer he could keep his lust under control, because wet or dry, angry or not, she was the most tempting female he had ever known.

He followed her out of the water. "I didn't mean to scare you," he said, sitting beside her. "Forgive me?"

"Maybe."

He lifted one brow. "Maybe?"

"For a kiss."

"I'll have to scare you more often," he murmured, before claiming her lips with his.

Later, they stretched out on the grass, side-by-side, while the warm sun dried their hair and clothing. "You've never mentioned your mother," Gryff remarked. "Is she still alive?"

"As far as I know. She ran away after my brother, Cobb, died. He was always her favorite. No one knows where she is."

"Where do you think she went?"

Marri shook her head. "I wish I knew."

"Why does your brother want you dead?"

She hesitated a moment, then said, "Because I'm next in line for the throne."

"Ah. Now it all makes sense." He thought a moment, then asked, "What about your father? Is he still alive?"

"He was when I left home."

Gryff dragged a hand across his jaw. Not only was she a princess; one day, she could very well be queen of Brynn Tor.

Marri sighed with regret as she climbed into the skiff. The two days they had spent in the glade were the happiest of her life. Gryff had taught her to swim. She had been reluctant at first, but there had been no way to resist his teasing smile. He swam in his trousers, she in her shift. She had been embarrassed at first, but he had soon put her at ease. They had spent the day by the lake, talking and napping, and swimming again before nightfall.

The next day they had taken a long walk through the tall grass. She had seen rabbits and squirrels and deer. To her amazement, the animals had not been afraid of them.

And now it was time to leave.

She glanced at Gryff as he climbed into the driver's seat. Already, her heart was aching at the thought of leaving him.

"You ready?" he asked.

"I guess so."

His gaze met hers. If he asked her to stay with him, would she say yes? Almost, he was tempted to ask. But he had nothing to offer her, nothing but a life on the run. She would never be safe with him as long as Serepta was alive…

Marri frowned. "What's wrong?"

"Nothing that hasn't been wrong from the start."

"I wish we could stay a little longer."

"Yeah. But we're almost out of food and water."

She couldn't argue with that.

She held onto the door handle as the skiff's engine roared to life. Moments later, they were speeding toward Tarnn.

CHAPTER 22

"Well, where are they?" Artur glared at Serepta as if it was her fault his sister was still missing, then returned to pacing the floor. "You said they were on their way here."

Serepta brushed an imaginary piece of lint from her cloak while she tried to decide whether to answer the impudent whelp or turn him into a wart hog. He had summoned her—*summoned her*—from her rooms at the inn as if she were one of his subjects.

"Well?" Artur paused again, hands fisted on his hips.

"It was my understanding they were coming here," she replied, her voice dripping frost. "Is there anywhere else they might go?"

"I thought she might have gone to Aisley Cloister, in Tarnn to visit her sister. I sent Dunnin to inquire after her sometime ago, but she wasn't there."

"Are you sure you can trust him?"

"Without doubt. He has served me well in the past."

"Perhaps you should send him again," Serepta remarked. "Just remember, the man with her is mine."

CHAPTER 23

Aisley Cloister crouched on top of a low rise like a lion about to pounce. Ancient trees lined the road to the entrance. Sunlight glinted off the stained-glass windows, danced across the surface of the stream that meandered down the hill and emptied into a lake that was perfectly round.

Marri had thought to feel some sense of relief when they arrived, a sense of anticipation at seeing her sister again. Once, taking shelter with the good sisters had seemed like the answer to all her problems. Now, she felt only despair. And it was all because of Gryff. She had spent her whole life behind walls of one kind or another; with Gryff, she had known freedom for the first time. True, she had also known fear and hunger. She had been imprisoned. Felt the sting of the lash. Seen cruelty in many forms. But none of that mattered now, not when he was going to leave her. If she asked him to stay with her, would he say yes?

She turned her head to look at him. His jaw was set, his expression impassive. By now, she knew him well enough to read his expressions, knew he had already made up his mind. He cared for her, she had no doubt of that, but he was going to leave her at the cloister because he felt she would be safer there.

They drove the rest of the way in silence.

Gryff parked the skiff a few yards away from the arched doorway. Came around to hand her out of the skiff. Walked her to the entrance. Rang the bell.

Several minutes passed before a rather plump woman clad in a black habit with a white wimple unlocked the door. "May I help you?"

"The lady here is seeking refuge with your order," Gryff said.

The nun looked at Marri, one brow raised.

"I believe my sister is here," Marri said. "Annis of Brynn Tor."

The nun inclined her head. "I am Sister Berrta." She took a step back. "Please come in."

Marri stepped inside.

Gryff followed her into a small, square room furnished with a long, low couch and a rectangular table. The walls were pale gray. A single, stained-glass window was set high in the pale gray wall.

"Please wait here while I inform Reverend Mother of your presence," Sister Berrta said.

Hands clasped, Marri sat on the edge of the sofa. Now that she was here, she longed to be anywhere else. And yet, she had no place to go. Gryff didn't want her. She couldn't go home.

She looked up as a tall, angular woman stepped into the room. Her gaze moved over Marri, missing nothing. "I am told you are seeking sanctuary."

Marri nodded.

"You are welcome here, of course, my child. Your sister has been informed and will join us shortly."

"Thank you, Reverend Mother."

The nun looked at Gryff for the first time. "Who are you?"

He shook his head. "No one of importance."

"I think you are important to Marri."

He lifted one shoulder and let it fall.

"We are in need of some temporary help," the nun remarked. "We cannot pay you, but we would provide you food and shelter."

Gryff glanced at Marri, saw the silent plea in her eyes.

"Mr. Gryff?"

"Just Gryff. Obliged for your offer, ma'am."

Reverend Mother smiled. It transformed her face, making her look much younger. "Ah, Sister Annis, please come in."

Marri jumped to her feet when her sister entered the room. For a moment, the two simply stared at each other. And then they fell into each other's arms.

Reverend Mother brushed a tear from her eye. After a moment, she said, "Sister Annis, why don't you take Marri to the dormitory and get her settled in the empty room next to yours. Gryff, if you'll come with me, I will show you to your quarters. You understand they are not within the cloister itself, but in the yard out back."

He nodded.

Marri broke her sister's embrace. "Gryff…"

"I'll be around for awhile," he said.

"You won't leave without telling me goodbye?"

"No." He would have hugged her, kissed her, save for the stern expression on the Reverend Mother's face.

Annis tugged on Marri's hand. With a last look at Gryff, Marri followed her sister out of the room.

Annis drew Marri down on the narrow cot. Clasping her sister's hands, she said, "Tell me everything."

Marri glanced around the room. White walls. A single window. A stone floor. The cot she sat on. A small table with a ewer and pitcher. It was even smaller than the skiff's cabin.

"Marri?"

"Artur sent Dakkar and Trist to kill me."

Annis stared at her, her face as white as her wimple. "Are you certain?" she asked, her voice a mere whisper.

"Yes."

"Talitha drugged me. Trist and Dakkar kidnapped me. I escaped, though I don't remember it, or anything that happened until Gryff took me in."

"Who is he? Gryff? He looks…scruffy and uncivilized."

"Perhaps he is but I don't care. I love him."

Mouth open, Annis blinked at her.

"Close your mouth," Marri said. "And I'll tell you all about it."

Gryff followed the tall nun down a wide hall, through a heavy door and out into the cloister's backyard. He didn't know what he'd expected, but it wasn't what he saw. The yard was large and divided in half by a wooden fence. One side contained a small barn, a corral that housed a brown-and-white cow, a chicken coop with perhaps a dozen chickens, a couple of pigs in a pen. A trio of goats regarded him from the top of what looked like a shed. A garden took up the other half of the yard.

He glanced at the nun. She stood with her arms folded, her expression thoughtful. "Something wrong?"

"Sometime back, a man came looking for Marri. He said her brother had sent him."

Gryff nodded. "Go on."

"I told him she hadn't been here, which was, of course, the truth. I didn't like the looks of the man. Is she in trouble?"

"More than you can imagine."

"I see."

"If you turn her away, she's got nowhere else to go," Gryff said flatly.

"Turning her away was never my intention, I assure you. I simply thought to warn you."

"Thanks, I appreciate it."

Reverend Mother nodded. "Put your fears aside. We will keep her safe." She cleared her throat. "As I mentioned before, we are in need of help. The young man who used to milk the cow and feed and water the stock ran off last month," she said. "The sisters look after the garden. Do you think you can care for the stock?"

"Sure, no problem."

"You'll sleep in there," she said, gesturing at the shed. "I think you'll find it comfortable.

Meals are at six, noon, and seven. You may take yours with us or in the kitchen. Is there anything you need?"

"Just a place to park the skiff. Preferably somewhere out of sight."

"There is another walled yard behind this one. I'll fetch the key to the gate."

Nodding, he followed her back into the convent, waited while she went into her office for the key, then continued out the front door.

As he drove around the back, he wondered how Marri's reunion with her sister was going.

"And so we came here." Marri sighed as she finished her tale. She had told her sister everything—well, almost everything.

"Weren't you scared to be alone with him? A total stranger? And that witch!" Annis shuddered. "I think I would have expired on the spot."

"It was scary, sometimes," Marri admitted. "But mostly it was exciting. As for Gryff, he's braver than any knight I ever knew. I wish...."

Annis shook her head. "You've changed, Marri. I hardly know you any more."

Marri nodded. Sometimes she hardly recognized herself. She had endured hunger and thirst, seen and done things she had never imagined. Fallen in love. No matter what the future held, if she spent another week with Gryff or only a day, he would always hold a place in her heart.

Chapter 24

Sitting back on her heels, Marri sent a rueful glance at the kitchen floor as she dipped a rag into a bucket of soapy water. Though she had only been at the cloister a day, it already seemed like forever. Idle speech was frowned upon, as was laughter. One wing of the cloister housed a number of aged and infirm women, many of whom could not feed or bathe themselves. In addition to caring for the bedridden, the nuns took turns cooking the meals, making bread, mopping and waxing the floors, washing the windows, doing the laundry, working in the garden, and a dozen other menial tasks.

Until she met Gryff, she had never done a day's work in her life. Her hands were sore, her back ached. She wasn't given to complaining, but going from a life of luxury to one of constant labor and self-denial wasn't going to be easy. There was, however, a certain satisfaction in looking after those who couldn't look after themselves. The nuns were kind. Her room, though small, was comfortable. The food was good. If not for Gryff, she might have resigned herself to spending the rest of her days in the convent, living a life of service and chastity. But not now. Gryff had spoiled her for any life that didn't include being in his arms.

Staring off into the distance, Gryff rested one arm on the top of the corral fence. As jobs went, this one wasn't looking too bad. He'd fed the stock, milked the cow, mucked out the stalls. With his chores finished, he glanced at the garden.

Hoping the nuns wouldn't mind, he passed an hour pulling weeds—an hour spent thinking of Marri. How, exactly, did the nuns spend their days? Surely they didn't devote all their time to prayer and meditation?

He couldn't imagine Marri happily living the rest of her life in the cloister. Clad in habit and wimple, he had hardly recognized her at breakfast. He had hoped to have a few minutes alone with her, but as soon as the meal was over, the nuns had filed silently out of the rectory, headed for the chapel.

At noon, a bell summoned him to the noon-day meal. He sat at a small table, apart from the sisters. It took him a minute to find Marri among the silent women. As though feeling his gaze, she glanced his way. She didn't look happy. Gryff held up two fingers, hoping she would get the message to meet him later that afternoon. A barely perceptible nod was his answer.

He was in the barn, currying a pretty chestnut mare, when Marri slipped inside.

Tossing the brush aside, Gryff opened his arms and she ran to him, her own arms wrapping around his waist.

For a moment, he didn't say anything, just held her close. Only one night apart and it seemed like a lifetime. He wanted to pull the wimple from her head and run his fingers through her hair, strip her of the shapeless habit and feast his eyes on the warm flesh beneath.

"Marri…"

"I know. I missed you, too."

"Are you happy here? Is this what you want?"

"No. I love being here with Annis, but….oh, Gryff," she wailed. "I want to be with you!"

"Marri, sweetheart…"

She placed her fingertips over his mouth with her hand, took a deep breath, and said in a rush, "I love you. I'll always love you. I don't want to be a princess or as queen. I…I just want to be your wife. Marry me, Gryff, and take me away from here." Seeing the argument rising in his eyes, she said, "If you don't marry me, I'll never marry anyone. I'll never know what it's like to make love to the man I adore. I…" Suddenly running out of steam, she fell silent, her hand falling to her side.

Gryff stared at her, momentarily speechless, and then swept her into his arms again. "I accept your proposal, princess."

Annis was shocked to hear that Marri intended to marry Gryff, a man without land or title. "What will father say?"

"I don't care. I love Gryff. I don't want to spend my life here. I want to be with him, have his children."

"But Artur…if what you say is true…"

"I don't care! Please, Annis, be happy for me."

At confession on Friday morning, Marri asked the visiting priest if he would perform the ceremony. At first, he refused. But when she vowed she would run away with Gryff and live in sin, the good father relented.

"Thank you, Father."

"I hope you do not regret marrying in haste, my child. Bring the young man here. I will marry you now."

She found Gryff in the barn.

He looked up, one brow lifting when he saw the bright smile on her face. Setting aside the harness he had been mending, he said, "What's got you looking so happy?"

"We're to be married! Now!"

"Now?" He frowned at her. "As in, right now?"

"Yes!" Her smile wavered. "Unless you've changed your mind?"

"Not a chance, sweetheart."

"Are you sure about this, child?" Reverend Mother asked as she helped Marri into a simple white shift.

"Yes, Mother. I love him with all my heart." Marri paused. "Will you give me your blessing?"

Reverend Mother shook her head. "I cannot see that any good will come of this. You are marrying outside the church, without your father's permission. I'm afraid I cannot condone your decision, but I do wish you every happiness."

Gryff stood at the altar, waiting for her. "Are you sure about this?" he whispered as she took her place beside him.

"Yes."

Holding hands, they exchanged the simple yet profound words that joined them as man and wife.

"You may kiss the bride," the priest said. "May God bless you both."

Marri gazed up at Gryff—her husband—as he drew her into his arms.

"I love you," he said fervently. "I will love you as long as I live."

"And I you."

Lowering his head, he kissed her ever so gently, wishing, fervently, that he had something more to offer her than all the love in his heart.

Now that Marri was a married woman, staying inside the cloister was no longer an option. She knew she should be appalled at the idea of spending her wedding night in the dilapidated shed where Gryff slept, but where they were didn't matter, as long as they were together. As long as she could be in his arms. She felt a little thrill of anticipation when he closed the door, locking out the rest of the world.

He lit several candles, then turned to face her. "Reverend Mother's been here," he remarked, gesturing at the colorful quilt that now covered the bed, the pillows, now covered with sparkling white cases. The simple white nightgown on the foot of the bed.

Marri nodded, her stomach in knots as Gryff drew her into his arms. Everything else melted away at his touch.

His gaze moved over her face, and then he kissed her ever so lightly. The fire that ignited from the mere brush of his lips across hers was hotter than the lava caves at Fennton. There was no need for foreplay, no need for words. Locked in each other's arms, they fell back on the bed, eager hands quickly shedding their clothing, touching, exploring. They came together in a rush as all the passion they had kept so tightly leashed exploded like a star going nova.

Marri clung to Gryff as the world she knew went up in flames. She was on fire, her whole body melting into his. She had never known what pleasure was until this moment, never knew the wonder of it, the sheer sensual power of joining her body with that of the man she loved.

For love him she did. Desperately.

He shuddered deep inside her, his face buried in her hair, his body trembling, damp with perspiration.

She stroked his back, her heart swelling with tenderness. Whatever happened in the future, she would forever cherish this moment. This man.

"Are you all right?" he asked his voice muffled.

"Never better."

He lifted on up his elbows. "Did I hurt you?"

"No. It was wonderful. Thank you."

He cocked one brow, then grinned. "No one's ever thanked me before."

Some of her euphoria faded. He was her first. How many had come before her? She knew about Serepta, of course, but had there been others? Women he hadn't been forced to bed?

"Marri?" His gaze searched her face. "What's wrong?"

She blinked furiously in an effort to stay her tears. "Nothing."

"You can't lie to me. I know you too well. Was it something I said? Something I did?"

Her gaze slid away from his. "Please, Gryff, let it go."

"Not until you tell me."

"You said no one's ever thanked you before."

"Yeah." He frowned at her, and then, as comprehension dawned, he swore softly. "I'm sorry, sweetheart. Would it help if I told you none of the others were ever important to me? Not the way you are."

"Only if you mean it."

He brushed his lips across her brow, the tip of her nose, her cheeks. His kisses were feather-light until he covered her mouth with his. He kissed her deeply, his tongue sweeping across her lower lip, dipping inside. When she was breathless, her hands clutching his shoulders, he lifted his head. "I meant it, love. Every word."

"Show me," she whispered. "Make be believe."

He gazed down at her, his eyes hot, his voice thick as he murmured, "My pleasure."

Marri sighed, her whole body aching in the most wonderful way. The first time had been amazing. This last time was beyond description. Gryff had made love to her slowly, arousing her, carrying her to the peak of ecstasy again and again. He had touched her and tasted her in ways that made her cry out with pleasure until, at last, he had carried her over the edge, leaving her spent and satisfied and more in love than ever.

She sighed again as he stood, let out a little shriek of surprise when he lifted her into his arms and carried her through a door she hadn't notice before and into a small bathroom with an equally small shower.

Standing under the spray, he found the soap and washed her from head to foot, then, with an expectant smile, he handed it to her.

Had anyone asked, Marri would have said making love was the most intimate thing a couple could do, but washing Gryff, soaping his arms and chest, his legs, that part of him that made him a man, was remarkably arousing.

Little wonder they wound up in bed yet again.

Gryff rolled onto his side, one arm across his brow. "Woman, you are insatiable."

"Me?" She punched him on the arm. "I didn't carry you out of the shower and into bed."

Trying hard not to laugh, he muttered, "Only because you couldn't lift me."

"Fine, then I'll never bathe you again."

"Okay, you win!" Grasping her around the waist, he pulled her onto his chest. "It was all my fault."

She laughed with the sheer joy of being in his arms, of knowing he was now hers for always, for forever. Laughed until he rolled over, his body covering hers, his mouth hot as he claimed her lips and her heart.

Gryff sat outside, his back braced against the side of the barn. Overhead, the twin moons silvered the land. How quickly his life had changed! If only his prospects had changed as well. He had nothing to offer Marri, couldn't think of anyplace that would provide a safe haven for the two of them. He had considered and rejected a dozen towns. If he could obtain a couple of fake travel orders, they could leave Brynn Tor, perhaps go to one of the moons. They'd be safe there.

Muttering an oath, he headed for his bed and his bride. He'd worry about the future tomorrow. Tonight, he wanted to be in his woman's arms.

Gryff was drifting toward sleep when something—a change in the air, a sound heard by his sub-conscious—jerked him from the brink. Rolling out of bed, he lifted his head, nostrils flaring as he tested the wind and scented danger lurking nearby.

He moved silently as he opened the door and stepped outside.

Shifting into the wolf, he sniffed the air again, growled softly as an unfamiliar scent filled his nostrils. He paused, his gaze searching the darkness. There, footprints leading from the convent to the back of the shed.

Head lowered, he trailed the scent, growled low in his throat when he saw the back door hanging open.

He padded quietly through the door, fear spiking through him when he heard Marri scream.

Inside the shed, a big brute of a man leaned over the bed, his hands wrapped around Marri's throat. A shock of white hair gave him a ghostly appearance.

With teeth bared, the wolf launched itself at the man's back, his teeth sinking deep into the artery in the man's neck.

With a roar, the man reared back, trying to shake off the wolf. Blood sprayed from the killing wound.

The wolf growled as he ripped out the attacker's throat. With a choked cry, the man fell backwards, ricocheted off the wall, staggered a few feet and crashed through the front door.

A gasp caught the wolf's attention. Looking up, he saw several nuns clad in their nightgowns running toward the shed. When they reached the doorway, they came to an abrupt halt, their eyes wide with horror and fear as they glanced from the dead man to the wolf.

Marri scrambled out of bed and hurried toward the door. "It's all right," she assured the nuns. "He won't hurt you. He's…he's a pet."

"A pet?" The Reverend Mother stepped warily into the room. "You brought a wolf here and didn't think to mention it?"

"I'm sorry, but I was afraid you wouldn't let him stay."

"You thought rightly." Reverend Mother's face paled as she glanced from the wolf to the body on the floor. She glanced at Gryff. "This is the man I told you about, the one who came looking for Marri."

"It's Dunnin," Annis said from the doorway. Face pale, she gave the wolf a wide berth as she hurried to Marri's side.

Reverend Mother nodded. "Yes, that was his name."

Marri shuddered. If she'd ever needed proof that her brother wanted her dead, she had it now. Trembling in the aftermath of the attack and the reality that her own flesh and blood had sent someone to kill her, Marri slumped on the edge of the bed, arms wrapped tightly around her middle.

Reverend Mother took a deep, calming breath. "The danger seems to be past, for now. We will talk more in the morning about your pet. Marri, where is your husband?"

"He heard something outside and went to check."

Reverend Mother nodded. "When he returns, please ask him to bury the body. Sisters, go back to bed. Annis, you may stay here until Gryff returns."

"Thank you, Mother."

Marri glanced at the wolf. "Go find Gryff."

With a short yip, he padded out of the room. Once out of sight, he resumed his own form.

Later, after making sure Marri was all right and sending Annis back to bed, Gryff found a shovel, then carried the dead man to a corner of the yard behind the garden and dumped him on the ground.

His fury against Marri's brother rode him hard as he dug the grave. What kind of monster ordered a hit on his own sister? Marri had said she had no designs on the throne. Surely she had told her brother that, as well. Apparently he hadn't believed her.

Gryff dropped the body into the hole and filled it in. Replaced the shovel in the barn. Washed his hands. And hurried back to his bride.

She was sitting up in bed, waiting for him, her face wan.

"Are you all right?"

"My throat's sore."

Sitting beside her, he examined her neck, felt his rage threaten to engulf him yet again when he saw the bastard's handprints on her pale skin. Damn the man! He wished he could kill him all over again.

Marri's gaze searched his. "We aren't safe here any more, are we?"

"No. We'll leave tomorrow."

"Where will we go?"

"Wherever the wind blows us, I guess."

Marri stared up at the ceiling, her thoughts in turmoil. Was there any place where they would be safe? Wherever they went, they would constantly be looking over their shoulders, wondering if every stranger they met was another of Artur's assassins.

There was, she thought, only one thing to do. Confront Artur face-to-face and swear to him by all she held dear that she didn't want the throne. If necessary, she would put it in writing.

She just hoped that, when all this was over, she and Gryff could spend the rest of their lives together in peace. Where they went didn't matter, as long as they were together.

CHAPTER 25

Artur paced from one side of the throne room to the other. Dunnin should have returned by now. Only death would prevent his favorite assassin's return.

Frowning, he paused to stare out the window. Dunnin possessed the strength and endurance of a young bull. It would take an incredibly strong man to defeat him.

He considered his other knights. None were as trustworthy or capable as his favorite.

Artur drummed his fingertips on the window frame. He would wait another day or two. If his assassin hadn't returned by then, he would go in search of Marri himself and dispatch her with his own two hands.

Serepta hurled the cauldron against the wall. It hit with a resounding thud, splashing water over the wall and the floor. She had tried every locator spell she knew. None of them had worked. And she knew the reason why. Seleena. What she didn't know was why her mother was interfering in something that was none of her business.

Perhaps it was time to find out.

It took only moments to prepare a new spell. A short incantation, a wave of her hand, and she was standing in front of Seleena's house in the dusty little village that had no name.

Seleena knew the exact moment when her daughter arrived at her door. There was no mistaking Serepta's dark magic. It poisoned the very air.

After taking a deep, calming breath to ground herself, she lifted the latch. "Good evening, daughter."

"Mother."

"What are you doing here?"

"Will you not invite me in?"

"I think not. What is it you want?"

Serepta's fangs flashed in a humorless smile. "I want to know why you are interfering in my life."

"Interfering? I don't know what you mean."

"You know exactly what I mean. How dare you conjure a protection spell for Gryff and his whore."

"I dare to do whatever I wish," Seleena retorted.

"He is mine."

"Yes, I saw the marks of your ownership on his flesh, sensed your evil on his soul."

"Do you know where he is?"

"No. Nor would I tell you if I did."

Serepta glared at her. "Remove the spell."

"I think not."

"Remove it!"

"I said no. You have no power here, my daughter. Be gone before I turn you into a nanny goat, or a yellow-backed newt."

Seleena crossed her arms over her breasts as Serepta summoned her power. She could almost see the darkness coalescing around her daughter, feel the strength and the anger building, smell the bloodlust that clung to her like rancid perfume.

It pained her to see her daughter—her once sweet and lovely child—so filled with hatred and vengeance. Unable to bear the sight any longer, Seleena stepped back and quietly closed the door.

Serepta had chosen the dark path; she must follow it to the end.

Hands tightly clenched at her sides, Serepta stared at the closed door. How was it possible for her mother to thwart her at every turn? Her dark magic should be stronger. Why wasn't it?

Pivoting on her heel, she stalked down the dusty street. Her only hope was that Gryff and the woman would return to Brynn Castle.

And if they didn't?

She shook her head. They would. They must.

She smiled as she kicked a cat out of her path. She had plans for her handsome slave and his whore. Protection spell or not, he was hers. He would always be hers. And if she couldn't have him, neither would anyone else.

CHAPTER 26

Marri glanced out the window of the Landskiff, her cheeks still damp from the tears she had shed when she bid farewell to Annis.

"We can visit her again, when this business with your brother is settled," Gryff said.

"I know." But knowing didn't ease the heartache she felt now. "Where are we going?"

"Back to Ironntown."

Surprised by his answer, she turned to look at him. "Do you think that's wise?"

"I'm betting your brother won't think of looking for us there again. Serepta knows where I used to live, but as far as I know, she's never heard of that tavern in Ironntown. We can hole up there unless we find a better place along the way."

Marri nodded. She still thought confronting Artur was the right thing to do, but Gryff had disagreed, insisting it was too dangerous.

Sighing, she glanced out the window again, praying they would find another haven, because she had no desire to return to that awful shack.

Darkness had fallen by the time they stopped for the night.

Stepping out of the skiff, Marri stretched her aching back before following Gryff around to the hatch. Thanks to the generosity of Mother Superior, they had enough food and water to last a few weeks.

Inside the cabin, she stood with arms akimbo, weary but not tired enough to sleep.

Her heart skipped a beat when Gryff came up behind her, his arms sliding around her waist as he nuzzled her neck. His breath was warm against her skin, his voice husky as he whispered her name.

She answered his unasked question by taking his hand and leading him toward her bed.

Warm anticipation engulfed her as they undressed each other. She never tired of looking at him, touching him. Sitting on the bed, she fell back on the mattress, tugging him down on top of her, welcoming his weight. She ran her hands over his back, remembering how Serepta had whipped him. How had he survived such cruelty? What would the witch do if she found him again?

"Hey, stop worrying." He smoothed the crease from her brow with his fingertips. "Everything will work out."

She wanted to believe him. Had to believe him. Because she couldn't bear to contemplate the consequences if he was wrong.

Gryff drove practically day and night until they reached Ironntown. Though Marri wasn't thrilled at returning, she was relieved that the journey was over.

They had made a brief stop at a space port. Using the credits Seleena had generously offered them, they bought a few changes of clothing, sheets, blankets and pillows, a large throw rug, and some personal items for Marri.

Gryff carried the carpet inside while Marri followed with the rest of their belongings.

She stood in the middle of the living room, appalled anew at what she saw.

"A coat of paint might help," Gryff suggested.

Marri nodded, then ducked through the curtain that divided the living room from the bedroom. Refusing to think of the past or the future, she stowed their new clothing in the scarred dresser, ripped the old linen from the bed, and smoothed the new sheets in place. After replacing the old pillow with two new ones, she gathered up the old bedding and carried it into the other room. "What should I do with this?"

"I'll get rid of it." He took it from her hands and carried it outside.

Sighing, she glanced around, wondering if they could buy a new sofa. Wondering how long they'd have to stay here. When she would see her sister again. Where her mother had gone.

When Gryff returned, she was still standing there.

"I don't know what I was thinking, to bring you back here. It's sure no place for a princess. Hell, it's hardly fit for the rats and the roaches."

Gathering her courage, Marri said, "I've been thinking."

"About?"

"Artur. I know you think it's too dangerous, but I'm certain the only way to end this is to confront him. I'm sure I can convince him that all I want to do is go away with you, and that if he agrees to let us go, he'll never see me again."

Gryff shook his head. "Do you really think he'll believe you?"

"I don't know. But what other choice do we have? I don't want to spend the rest of my life waiting for another of his assassins to find me."

Heaving a sigh, Gryff drew Marri into his arms, a surge of protectiveness sweeping through him when she rested her head on his chest. Hard to believe he had once thought of her as a burden; now, he couldn't imagine his life without her.

Long after Marri had fallen asleep, Gryff continued to think about what she'd said about confronting Artur, but taking her back home seemed like an incredibly bad idea. From what he knew of her brother, it seemed unlikely Artur would blithely accept her promise to leave and wish her well. And while Gryff wasn't afraid of a fight, it would be suicide for one man to go against Artur's army.

And then there was Serepta. Always Serepta.

Damn and blast! What the devil was he going to do about her?

CHAPTER 27

Artur slammed his fist against the wall. Time was running out. His father had taken to his bed. It was only a matter of weeks, perhaps a month, before the old man passed on. According to the law of the land, Artur could not be proclaimed king until there was proof that Marri was dead or incapable of ruling the kingdom. He could rule in her absence, but only as Prince Regent.

Serepta proclaimed to be a powerful witch, but so far, Marri had eluded her magic.

Well, she wasn't the only witch in the land. Summoning his page, he said, "Send one of the knights to summon Nardik."

If Serepta couldn't locate Marri, perhaps his father's wizard could.

Nardik swept into the Great Hall, his cloak billowing behind him. He did not bow to Artur, merely inclined his head, as if he considered himself to be of equal—if not greater—rank than royalty. "You wished to see me?" He spoke quietly, yet his voice carried to the furthest corner of the room.

"Yes," Artur said. "Thank you for coming so quickly."

"How may I be of service?"

"My sister has been missing for quite some time. I am worried for her safety. I was hoping you could locate her for me."

"I will need something that belongs to her. An item of clothing would be best."

Artur snapped his fingers and a page ran up the stairs.

Artur frowned when Serepta entered the Hall. "I don't recall sending for you."

"Forgive me, majesty," she said, "but I sensed the presence of another witch."

"Ah. This is my father's wizard, Nardik."

"Indeed?" There was no mistaking the disdain in Serepta's voice as she regarded the wizard. He was tall and thin, but not spindly. Long gray hair framed a narrow face with flat cheeks, an aquiline nose, and eyes the color of honey.

Nardik looked down his nose at her. "Seleena's daughter." He nodded, his expression one of barely veiled contempt. "Magic wasn't enough for you, so you sought the Dark Gift. Has it served you well?"

"Well enough!"

"Yet you cannot accomplish a simple location spell."

"They are under my mother's spell of protection!"

He snorted disdainfully.

Re-entering the room, the page knelt in front of Nardik, a dark blue glove in his hand.

Nardik took it from him, laid it on a nearby table, and bowed his head. Power flooded the room as he uttered an incantation.

It was one Serepta had never heard, but she knew it was working. She could feel it in every fiber of her being. Jealousy knifed through her. How could this man—this wizard—control more power than did she? The vampire who had turned her had promised that her magic would be stronger than that of any other witch, wizard, or sorcerer. She clenched her fists. He had lied to her. That was the only answer.

The wizard's power swelled, reached a crescendo, and dissipated. "Your sister is in Ironntown.'

Brow knit, Artur asked, "Are you certain?"

"You doubt me?"

"No, never." Artur shook his head. "I did not think they would go back there. I will send a dozen of my knights after them at once."

"It will take them days to get there," Nardik remarked. "I can be there and back by morning."

Artur smiled, pleased.

"I'm going with you," Serepta declared.

"I travel alone," the wizard said, and his tone left no room for argument. Gathering his cloak around him, he vanished.

CHAPTER 28

Unable to sleep, Gryff shifted into the wolf and stalked the night. But for once, he couldn't put the worries of the day behind him. Taking Marri home still seemed like an incredibly bad idea. Serepta knew about Artur. If the two joined forces…

He growled deep in his throat. He didn't even want to think of such an eventuality. He needed to find a place for Marri, somewhere no one would ever think to look for them. Off-planet was the only solution. It wouldn't be easy to find transport from Brynn Tor. He would need a disguise. So would Marri. Then there were travel papers, passports, cash...

He was nearing the shack when an unfamiliar scent reached his nostrils. Slowing, he padded silently toward the front door, hackles raising when he realized there was a stranger inside the house. Supernatural power rippled across his skin.

"Come in, wolf."

The voice—male—compelled him to cross the threshold.

The stranger smiled at him. "A shapeshifter." He clapped his hands. "I didn't know there were any left on Brynn Tor. Gryff, is it?"

The wolf growled.

"Marri is in the other room," the wizard said. "She is unhurt, and will remain that way, as long as you cooperate."

With a shake of his head, Gryff resumed his own form, only to find he couldn't move. Damn and blast. More witchcraft. "What do you want?"

"Can you transform into other beasts?" the wizard asked. "Other beings?"

"When I want to," Gryff replied curtly. "What do you want?"

"I've come to take the two of you to Brynn Castle."

"Returning means death for Marri."

After a moment's hesitation, the wizard said, "That is not my concern."

There was no emotion in the wizard's voice, no hope of changing his mind, so Gryff didn't bother trying. "Why are you doing this?"

"It is Artur's wish."

"Why do you care what he wants?"

"I have aligned myself with the royal family. I find it lucrative in many ways."

"So it's all about the money?"

The wizard shrugged. "Artur's father is my friend. I do not have many."

"Yeah? Well, you're about to lose the one you have."

A flicker of emotion slid behind the wizard's eyes. "Explain."

"Artur intends to murder his sister, and then his father, so that he can rule Brynn Tor."

"You have proof of this?"

"You're a wizard! Can't you discern a lie?"

"I've heard nothing of the king's illness."

Gryff shrugged. "Of course not. If you knew he was ailing, you might have healed him. Artur wouldn't want that."

"What are you to Serepta?"

Just her name sent an icy chill down Gryff's spine. "Is she there?"

"Yes. Waiting for you."

"I was her slave. In her mind, I belong to her. I have the scars to prove it."

"She was once a lovely young thing, but she has perverted her gift. Sooner or later, it will destroy her."

"Not soon enough."

"I told Artur I would have you back by morning. You will spend the night here. I will return at dawn." The wizard murmured an incantation. "You will not be able to leave the house. I suggest you spend this night with the woman. You might not get another."

Marri looked up when Gryff pushed the curtain aside. A wordless cry rose in her throat as she slid off the bed and into his arms.

She stood there a moment before murmuring, "Not long ago, I wished Nardik was with me."

"Looks like you got your wish," he muttered.

"I never thought he'd turn against me. When I was a little girl, he entertained me with magic tricks for hours. On my fifth birthday, he conjured a unicorn for me. Oh, Gryff, what are we going to do?"

"You wanted to talk to your brother. It looks like you're going to get your chance." Taking her by the hand, he moved to the bed. Sitting on the edge of the mattress, he pulled her onto his lap, one hand idly stroking her back. "Whatever happens, I'm glad you wandered into my tavern."

"Are you? Even though I've brought you nothing but trouble?"

"You're no trouble, sweetheart."

"I love you so much."

"I love you, too, wife." Cupping her face in his palms, he whispered, "You'll never know how much." And kissed her.

Marri melted against him as his tongue plundered her mouth. His hands caressed her. And even as she surrendered to his touch, his words repeated in her mind—*I love you, too, wife*. Truly, the sweetest words she had ever heard.

He pressed her back on the mattress, eased her out of her clothing, cast his aside.

She thought briefly of Nardik—what were his intentions? But Gryff's caresses swept worries of the future from her mind. This might be the last time he held her in his arms, the last time she could touch him and taste him. The last time…she gasped with pleasure as their bodies came together, straining, reaching, grasping for that one instant when two truly became one—heart and soul, mind and body.

She felt the sting of tears when, at the moment of climax, he whispered again that he loved her. Would always love her.

In the morning, Marri feigned sleep as long as possible, wanting to spend every moment she could in Gryff's arms. But, all too soon, Nardik was there, demanding they prepare to leave.

Any hope she'd had of making some kind of miraculous escape vanished when Nardik wrapped them in one of his magic spells and whisked them off to the throne room of Brynn Castle.

She screamed Gryff's name when one of Nardik's spells sent him to the dungeon.

"Really, sister, that is most unladylike."

"You!" She whirled on her brother like a bear defending her cubs. "Why are you doing this? I don't want the throne! I've told you that again and again. Why won't you believe me?"

"I wish I could."

"It's true! Just let me go away with Gryff and you'll never see me again."

"I'm afraid that's impossible. I've promised him to the witch. Serepta."

"No." Marri shook her head. "No."

Artur summoned one of his guards with a wave of his hand. "Take her to her rooms. Make sure she doesn't leave. It will be your head if you fail me."

"Yes, majesty."

"Please, Artur…"

"Be gone!"

Marri squared her shoulders. Lifted her chin. And marched up the winding staircase to her room. Only when she was safely behind closed doors did she let the tears fall.

"She's telling the truth, you know," Nardik remarked. "She doesn't want the throne."

"That may be true today, but what about tomorrow? Next month? Next year?"

"I am not a prophet. I cannot see her future. But I can see yours."

Artur's head jerked up. "What does that mean?"

"It means if you harm a hair on that child's head, you will not live long enough to regret it."

Artur shook his head, eyes wide with disbelief. "You dare threaten me?"

"I would not call it that."

"What would you call it?"

"A promise. I have no children of my own, nor do I want any. But I watched Marri grow up. I will not see her robbed of her future. You would be wise to let her go away with her young man. If you keep her here, if any harm befalls her, I will hold you responsible."

Speechless, Artur could only stare at him. And then, in a blinding blue flash, the wizard was gone. But his words lingered in the air, like smoke.

If any harm befalls her, I will hold you responsible.

Chilled to the marrow of his bones, Artur paced the floor, Nardik's threat hanging over his head like the sword of doom. Damn the man! Who'd have guessed that, under that stern exterior, the wizard harbored a soft spot for Marri? What if she really was telling the truth? What if he let her leave Brynn Castle with the promise never to return?

Could he count on his sister to keep her word?

Did he have any other choice?

He slapped a hand to his brow. Of course! He would have her renounce the throne in front of the knights and the villagers, as well as the leading brethren of the church, and proclaim that he, Artur, was the sole heir to the throne. . A vow like that, spoken before highborn and peasant alike, could not be recanted. Why hadn't he thought of it before?

Feeling like a fool, he shook his head. He'd been so focused on dispatching Marri, he had overlooked the most obvious solution

Pleased to have solved the problem, he ran up the stairs to tell her the good news.

When Artur reached Marri's room, the knight guarding the door came to attention. Artur brushed past him, his excitement smothered by a sudden sense of impending doom when he lifted the latch.

The chamber was empty.

CHAPTER 29

Gryff regained consciousness slowly. He didn't have to open his eyes to know where he was. The cold stone floor, the dampness, the combined stink of old blood and sweat and urine were all too familiar.

He groaned softly as he sat up. Damn Serepta. Had she spirited him out of Brynn Castle with no one the wiser? Or had Artur given her the okay? Either way, he was back in hell. He rubbed a hand across his jaw. Had she taken Marri, too?

He called the witch's name, felt his gut tighten when he called it again and there was no answer.

Where was she?

Rising, he paced the floor, his agitation growing as his imagination painted one horrible possibility after another—Marri was dead. She had been given to Serepta's henchmen. She had been tossed in a pit and left to die. She was in Serepta's torture chamber, her hands bound to the iron rod over her head, being beaten, whipped, slowly bleeding to death.

"Serepta!" He roared the witch's name.

"You called?" She appeared outside his cell in a puff of smoke.

"Where is she?"

The witch smiled. There was no warmth in it. "On her way to the slave auction in Bosquetown. She should fetch a pretty price, don't you think?"

Gryff's hands fisted around the bars. "Bring her back."

"Why would I do that?"

"Please." He hissed the word through clenched teeth.

"Are you willing to beg for her life?"

He dropped to his knees, bowed his head. "Please spare her."

"And if I agree? What will you give me in return?"

"Whatever you want."

"Your loyalty. Your promise not to escape again, and to make love to me often of your own free will. Your presence at my side every day and night as long as you draw breath."

"And you'll let her go wherever she wishes?"

"Will you do as I ask?"

"Yes."

"Swear it on her life."

He answered without hesitation. "I swear."

"Very well."

Still kneeling, he looked up at her. "I'll want proof that you've kept your part of the bargain."

"When she returns from Bosquetown, I will bring her here so you can see she is unhurt, and then my mother can take her home, or anywhere she desires to go. Does that suit?"

Gripping the bars in both hands, Gryff pulled himself to his feet. "One more thing. I don't want Marri tortured or imprisoned while we wait for your mother."

"I promise she will be treated like the princess she is."

"And after Seleena takes her home, I want her to come back and tell me to my face that Marri is safe."

"Anything else?" Serepta asked, her voice laced with impatience.

"I guess not."

"Just remember, my pet, if you break your word, she will suffer for it. I promise you that her death will be slow, and you will watch every agonizing moment."

"I believe you."

Serepta nodded. "Then we have an accord." With a wave of her hand, the witch was gone.

Resting his forehead against the bars, Gryff closed his eyes. He had little choice but to take Serepta at her word. He had far more faith in Seleena.

Whispering Marri's name, he sank down on the cold stone floor.

He would never be free again, but it didn't matter, as long as Marri was safe.

Marri sat in a corner of a large room, her fingers nervously worrying a lock of her hair, her heart pounding with fear. Around her, dozens of other young girls and women chattered nervously. Hundreds of men from all over the galaxy circled the floor, their eyes avidly darting from one woman to another.

She was going to be sold as a slave.

As terrifying as that thought was, she was more worried about Gryff. He was Serepta's prisoner again. No matter how horrible her life as a slave might be, being the witch's prisoner would be even worse.

Her nerves grew taut as, one by one, the other girls were auctioned off to the highest bidder.

It took hours, as each girl was paraded back and forth.

She huddled deeper into the corner, trembling uncontrollably, as the number of women dwindled. If she revealed the secret of her true identity to her new master with the promise of a reward to return her to Brynn Tor, would he believe her? Or laugh in her face?

She looked up, feeling as though she might faint, as one of the men in charge of the auction pulled her to her feet and dragged her to the front of the room. He had just started to describe her attributes when another man stepped up beside her.

"The Lady Serepta is withdrawing this one." He didn't wait for a response, merely grabbed Marri's arm and hustled her outside and into the back of a familiar transport.

Marri slumped against the side of the vehicle, not knowing whether to be frightened or relieved.

Gryff caught her scent before she entered the dungeon. Rising, he raked his fingers through his hair, straightened his clothing, and moved toward the front of the cell.

"Marri." He whispered her name as she hurried toward him.

"Gryff!" She slipped her arms through the gaps in the bars and hugged him as best she could. "I was so afraid!"

His gaze searched hers. "Are you all right?"

"Yes, I'm fine. But you…" Tears glistened in her eyes. "We have to get you out of here."

Shaking his head, he took her hands in his. "I promised I'd stay, that I'd do whatever she wanted, as long as she released you. You're free to go home or wherever you want."

"Not without you."

"Marri, she's won."

"I refuse to believe that!"

"Seleena's going to take you home, if that's your choice. I trust her."

Marri stared at him, unable to believe what she was hearing. He had voluntarily given up his freedom—his life—for her. How could she accept that?

"Be happy, sweetheart."

"How can I, knowing you're here? I love you."

"I know." He caressed her cheek, his gaze moving over her face, committing it to memory—the softness of her skin, the deep blue-green of her eyes, the tilt of her nose, the lush fullness of her lower lip. He would never forget her, never regret bargaining with Serepta for Marri's life. "I love you, princess. Go live the life you were meant to have."

"Gryff…"

"Go on, get out of here."

She hesitated, as if she would argue; then, head held high, she walked away, her bearing regal, every inch a princess.

Heart heavy, throat thick with tears he refused to shed, he watched her until she was out of sight.

Marri had no sooner left the dungeon than Serepta appeared. A wave of her hand unlocked his cell. Beckoning for him to follow her, she made her way up the stairs and down the long, narrow corridor to her chambers.

Feeling like a condemned man on his way to the gallows, Gryff trailed in her wake. He had only one thought in mind—to destroy her, even if it cost him his own life.

She ordered him to bathe, clothed him in a pair of tight-fitting black leather pants and nothing more.

He stood before her, feeling dirtier than he ever had in his life, as she reclined on her bed.

"It's time to make good on your promise."

He didn't have to ask which one she meant. Stretching out on the bed, he closed his eyes and drew her into his arms.

Marri sat in the front parlor, her hands tightly folded in her lap. One of Serepta's servants had told her she was to wait there for Seleena. After warning her not to leave the room, the servant departed, closing the door behind her.

Marri's foot tapped impatiently on the plush carpet. How could she leave Gryff in this dreadful place? There had to be a way to free him. Did he honestly think she could just forget the vows they had exchanged and go off and enjoy the rest of her life knowing he had sacrificed his to save her?

She wasn't a fool. There was no way she could hope to defeat Serepta on her own. But...

Marri looked up when the door opened and Seleena entered the room.

"Are you ready to go?" the witch asked. "My daughter informed me that I was to take you anywhere you wished."

"Home," Marri said. "I want to go home."

Marri's spirits lifted as she followed Seleena out of the castle. Serepta's mother had helped them once before. Maybe she would again.

CHAPTER 30

Marri's enthusiasm for home waned as they crossed the moat to Brynn Castle. Why had she come here?

Gathering her courage, she swept into the Great Hall. She was tired of being afraid. She had every right to be here. The throne was rightfully hers, if she wanted it. But right now, she had more important things on her mind. Seleena was a powerful witch, but why fight Serepta with one witch when she had two? Nardik had never refused her anything. Surely he would help her now.

"Marri."

She glanced over her shoulder at the sound of Artur's voice. "I don't have time to argue with you now," she said. "Gryff needs my help."

"This won't take long. If you will publicly renounce your right to the throne, you may live here in peace for as long as you wish."

"Whatever you want. But later. I need Nardik. Where is he?"

"I am here, child."

Marri looked to her right and saw him standing beside Seleena. Not exactly standing. They were in each other's arms.

Marri darted a glance at Artur, one brow raised.

He shook his head, his expression as surprised as hers certainly was. "I say, what's going on here?"

Nardik lifted his head. "Seleena and I are old friends." He smiled down at her. "Very old friends." After a moment, he focused on Marri. "What did you want?"

"Gryff is being held in Serepta's castle. I was hoping you and Seleena could help me free him."

Sadness tugged at Nardik's features. "I fear she will never change."

"I fear you are right," Seleena agreed.

"Perhaps it is time to revoke her magic."

Seleena nodded.

"Can you do that?" Marri asked. "Take away her magic?"

Wrapping one arm around Seleena's shoulders, Nardik turned to face Marri. "We gave it to her. We can take it away."

"Will she still be a vampire?"

"Yes. Until now, her magical powers have allowed her to walk in daylight, to eat and drink mortal food. But once her magic is gone, she will be forced to live as a vampire, with all that it entails."

Marri shuddered at the thought. "How soon can we leave?"

"Whenever you wish."

"Then what are we waiting for? Let's go!"

Staring up at the ceiling, Gryff listened to the slow, even breathing of the woman beside him. One day as her prisoner and it already felt like a lifetime.

Rolling onto his side, he propped himself on one elbow. She was a beautiful woman, as beautiful as she was evil. He lifted his right hand, imagined it curled around her throat. Could he choke the life out of her before she woke? Or, better yet, shift into the wolf and rip out her black heart.

It would be murder. Cold-blooded murder.

How could he go to Marri with another woman's blood—even Serepta's blood—on his hands?

He stared at her throat, imagined his fingers tightening around it, slowly squeezing the life from his body…

The next thing he knew, he was back in his cell in the dungeon.

Gryff bolted upright, all his senses alert. He hadn't seen Serepta or anyone else since the witch spirited him back to his cell last night. Had she somehow divined his murderous thoughts? Damn and blast. Had he put Marri's life in danger again?

He thrust the question aside as, eyes narrowed, he probed the darkness. Seeing nothing, he shifted into the wolf. There! Three dark shapes ghosting down the pitch-black corridor toward him. Marri! Her scent filled his nostrils. What the hell was she doing back here?

Snuffling, he caught Seleena's scent.

The tall man beside her was a stranger.

A low growl rose in the wolf's throat as the trio reached his cell. The man waved his hand, and the torch set high in the wall flickered to life.

"Hurry," Seleena whispered. "We don't have much time."

The man threw her a smile. "Patience, woman. We have all the time we need." He murmured something in a language the wolf didn't recognize. A moment later, the cell door swung open.

With a wordless cry, Marri rushed into the cell and threw her arms around the wolf's neck.

He shook her off, then resumed his own shape. "Are you out of your mind? What are you doing here?"

"We came to rescue you, you ungrateful beast."

"Yeah, well you're too late. She's here."

The man pushed Marri into the cell and put Seleena behind him, then turned to face Serepta.

She paused an arm's length away. "Mother, how nice to see you."

Seleena inclined her head but said nothing.

"If you've come for Gryff, you're wasting your time," Serepta said. "He gave me his word he would stay here. So, be gone, all of you. Unless you wish to join him." She stared at the man, her brows drawn in a frown. "Have we met?"

He nodded. "On the day you were born."

Her frown deepened.

"I am Nardik."

Her eyes widened. Evidently she had heard of him, Gryff thought.

Serepta's gaze moved from Nardik's face to her mother's and back again.

The wizard nodded. "Yes. I'm your father. And you, my dear daughter, are going to release this man from his promise."

Serepta made a dismissive gesture with her hand. "What right do you have to come here and dictate what I will do? Father!" She spat the word. "I have no father!"

"Do not defy me," he warned.

"I'm not afraid of you!"

Gryff felt Serepta gathering her power as she spoke. It raised the hairs at his nape, made the hairs on his arms stand at attention. He grabbed Marri and backed deeper into the cell as the room grew thick with magic.

Oblivious to whatever spell his daughter was conjuring, Nardik grabbed Serepta by the arm and jerked her toward him.

Serepta tore free of her father's grasp. Bodies rigid, they stared at each other, a silent duel raging between them. Sparks exploded through the air. It was, Gryff thought, a literal battle between good and evil.

Serepta was rumored to be the most powerful witch in the land. Watching the battle, Gryff feared the rumors might be true. He could feel her evil magic crawling over his skin.

Eyes blazing, Nardik hissed, "Now!" He lunged forward, his cloak folding around Serepta like the wings of a large black bird until it covered her from head to heel. Seleena rushed forward at the same time, her arms wrapping around Nardik and their daughter.

Power seethed in the room as the three witches struggled.

As if someone had turned a switch, the air stilled.

Marri looked up at Gryff. "What's happening?"

He shook his head. "Beats the hell out of me." He drew Marri closer as Seleena backed up a few steps. Nardik's cloak fell away. He stood straight and tall, his dark eyes alight.

Gryff frowned. Serepta looked the same, and yet…something was different.

"What have you done?" Serepta stared at her parents. "What have you done?" She screamed the words.

"Deprived you of your gift," Nardik said, his voice as cold as the stone floor. "You have abused it long enough."

"No! No, that's impossible!"

"I am sorry," Nardik said quietly. "Seleena, let us depart." Taking Seleena's hand, he turned to go.

Serepta stood there, her expression blank. And then, eyes filled with rage, she lunged at Gryff, fangs bared, her hands like claws.

With a growl, Gryff shoved Marri out of the way, shifted to the wolf, and sprang at the vampire's throat. He was bigger, stronger, and he drove her backward, landing on top of her when she hit the floor. Burying his teeth in her throat, he shook his head.

Blood sprayed from the killing wound, staining the floor, the walls, his muzzle.

When he was sure she was dead, he backed away. Lifting his head, he stared at Nardik and Seleena.

The wizard nodded. "We'll wait for you outside."

Uncertain of what Marri's reaction would be, Gryff hesitated a moment before resuming his own shape, then slowly turned toward her.

Marri blew out a sigh. Ripping a piece of material from Serepta's skirt, she wiped the blood from his face. "Let's go home."

When they arrived at Brynn Tor, a page hurried to summon Marri's brother from his private chamber.

Artur entered the Great Hall wearing a white shirt, baggy brown trousers, and his favorite forest green cloak. Taking his place on the throne, his gaze moved over Marri and Gryff before settling on the wizard. "So, Nardik, I see you have brought them all safely home."

"Yes," the wizard said. "And a surprise, as well."

"A surprise?" Artur leaned forward, looking as eager as a child awaiting a treat. "What might that be?"

With a wave of his hand, Nardik opened the door on the north side of the Hall.

An audible gasp erupted from Artur's throat when he saw his father—and the woman standing at his side.

"Mama." Marri's eyes filled with tears as her parents entered the room.

When Amerris opened her arms, Marri ran to her. With tears running down her cheeks, she embraced her mother. She had a hundred questions to ask, but none of them seemed important now.

"How I've missed you." Amerris stroked her daughter's hair.

"Where have you been?"

"Not far. Nardik kept me informed about things happening here. When he told me you intended to renounce the throne, I knew I had to come home. I will not let that happen, daughter. I will not let Artur sit on the throne of Brynn Tor."

"Here, now," Leonid said, glancing from one to the other. "What are you talking about?"

Amerris pointed an accusing finger at her son. "Ask him. Ask him for the truth of what happened to his brothers. Or why Annis ran away in fear for her life. And Marri, too. Ask him!"

Marri looked at Artur, watched him shrink at their mother's accusations.

Leonid snorted with disdain. "Did Marri fill your head with this nonsense? She came to me with the same wild stories, claiming Artur killed Caddor and Cobb."

"And you didn't believe her."

"How could I?"

Amerris shook her head. "Artur was always your favorite. When he was a child, you turned a blind eye to his cruelty, refused to believe any who spoke against him. But it was all true. When he killed Cobb, I could no longer stay here with him. Or with you."

Leonid approached the throne. "Tell me," he said, his voice ringing off the walls. "Tell me the truth!"

Artur shook his head. "Lies!" he shouted. "It's all lies!"

Leonid glanced over his shoulder. "Nardik?"

"Amerris speaks the truth. It is the boy who lies."

"Artur," the king said quietly. "Tell me the truth."

Eyes blazing maniacally, he screamed, "I did it! I killed them all! The throne is mine!" Pulling the jeweled dagger from the sheath at his side, Artur sprang at his father. His aim was true. The blade buried itself to the hilt in the king's heart.

Marri screamed, "No!" as her father dropped to his knees, one hand clutching his chest.

Gryff ran forward, intending to put himself between Artur and Marri. He was halfway there when Nardik conjured a lance from midair and hurled it at Artur.

It buried itself in his back.

With a cry of pained surprise, the boy who would be king fell dead at his father's feet.

Amerris covered her face with her hands.

Marri stared at her brother, seeing him as he had been so many years ago—a happy baby, a curious toddler, an energetic little boy.

What had changed him into the man he had become?

Turning away, she buried her face against Gryff's chest and let her tears flow.

Feeling numb, Marri stood at the window of her bedchamber. Night had fallen and the castle lay quiet beneath a pair of bright yellow moons. Everything had happened so fast, she was still trying to sort it out in her mind.

Gryff had killed Serepta. Marri had tried to feel at least a hint of regret at the witch's death, but it was impossible. The woman had been evil inside and out.

Artur was dead, killed by Nardik. The thought brought a wave of fresh tears. Again, she tried to summon some sense of loss and failed. Her tears were not for Artur, but for Caddor and Cobb, for the years of pain and suffering that Artur's obsession with the throne had caused their family.

Her father was dead, killed by his own son. Grief shredded her heart. Her father might yet be alive if he had listened when she tried to warn him about Artur.

Earlier, she had inquired as to Talitha's whereabouts, only to learn that her former chambermaid had fled the castle moments after Marri returned. A wise decision, Marri thought. She had no sympathy for the woman who had betrayed her.

She dried her tears when someone knocked at the door. Sensing her wish to be alone, Gryff had left the castle, no doubt to go running beneath the full moon. Expecting his return, she called, "It's open. Come in."

Amerris, attired in deep mourning, stepped into the room and closed the door behind her.

"How are you, daughter?"

"I'll be all right." Marri forced a smile. "I'm so glad you've come home."

Amerris sat on the edge of the bed and patted the mattress beside her. "Come, sit with me. We have much to discuss."

Alarmed by her mother's tone, Marri perched on the edge of the mattress.

Amerris took Marri's hand in hers. "I'm sorry I left you. I never should have run away, but I didn't know what else to do. I knew Artur had killed his brothers, that he intended to have the throne at any cost, but I never thought he would turn on you. I've always known you had no desire to rule, and I was confident Artur knew it, as well." She shook her head. "I still cannot believe a son of mine was capable of such despicable acts."

In lieu of words, Marri squeezed her mother's hand. They sat in silence for several moments before Marri spoke. "Have you been with Nardik all this time?"

"Yes." Amerris gazed out the window a moment before she said, "We intend to marry when the mourning period is over."

Marri stared at her mother in disbelief. And then she frowned. "But....what of Seleena? He fathered her child."

Amerris smiled faintly. "They've been friends a very long time. Serepta was conceived in a brief moment of passion."

"You and Nardik." Marri shook her head. "However did it happen?"

Amerris shrugged. "Does anyone ever know? All I do know is that I don't want to live without him." She took a deep breath and exhaled slowly. "You have much to consider now. You must be crowned Queen as soon as possible. I know you've always held Nardik in high regard, and I would suggest you appoint him as your chief advisor. He is a wise man, one you can trust."

Marri nodded, though she was still trying to wrap her mind around the fact that her mother was in love with the wizard. But the more she thought about it, the more pleased she became. Her parents had never been in love, never been happy together. Theirs had been a marriage to unite kingdoms, not hearts.

"Now, what of this man, Gryff?" Amerris asked briskly. "What is he to you?"

"He is my Nardik," Marri replied with a quiet smile. "I love him more than my life."

"But he is a commoner!" her mother exclaimed, aghast at the very idea.

"I know."

"Child, it simply isn't done. You're the queen now, you must marry royalty."

"I'm afraid it's too late for that."

Amerris frowned. "What do you mean?"

"Gryff is my husband."

Amerris stared at her. After a moment, she said, "The marriage must be annulled immediately."

"No."

Amerris considered trying to change her daughter's mind, but, hearing the steel beneath the softly-spoken refusal, she knew it was pointless. "You could knight him," she remarked, thinking out loud. "And then grant him land in the northern part of Brynn Tor. That would give him status."

"Sir Gryff," Marri said, and burst out laughing. "I can't wait to tell him!"

The wolf raced through the forest behind the castle, trying to empty his mind of everything but the hare he was chasing. But, for once, there was no solace in the night, no forgetting that Marri would soon be queen of Brynn Tor, and when that happened, all his dreams of spending his life with the woman he loved would be swallowed up in reality.

He had nothing to offer Brynn Tor's new ruler—not power, not wealth, not land. Not a damn thing. She would be forced to dissolve their marriage. Wed a man worthy of her. Share his bed. Bear his children...

With a growl, the wolf's jaws closed on the rabbit's throat. A quick shake broke the creature's neck. Blood filled his mouth. Suddenly repulsed, he tossed the furry corpse aside.

No matter how he longed to share his life with her, Marri would forever be out of his reach.

Marri paced the floor of her chamber. Where was Gryff? He had been gone for hours. Had something dreadful happened to him?

She was giving serious thought to sending the royal guard out to search for him when he entered the room.

"Gryff! I've been so worried. Where have you been?"

"Nothing for you to fret about, princess. I just needed a little fresh air. Everything okay here?"

"As much as it can be. I've so much to do. I need to let the people know that their king is...is gone, and..."

"You'll be fine. You were born to be queen. With Artur out of the way…" He shrugged.

"All your problems are solved."

"My mother's in love with Nardik."

He grunted softly. "I didn't see that coming."

"Nor did I. They plan to wed next year."

He nodded. "I wish you well, Marri."

Alarmed by the tone of his voice, she frowned. His expression was implacable. "Gryff…"

"Hey, you're the queen now. You don't need a guy like me in your life. I'd just be an embarrassment to you."

"You're leaving me?" Feeling as though all the air had been sucked out of the room, she stared up at him. "But…"

"I don't belong here and we both know it."

Determined not to cry, Marri lifted her head, blinked back her tears. She was Queen of Brynn Tor. If he wanted to leave, then good riddance. She didn't need him.

But she did. More than her next breath. "I forbid you to go."

His eyes narrowed. "Is that right?"

"I am your wife, Gryff Donovan. But even more than that, I am your queen. As such, I command you to stay here. If you refuse, I'll…I'll…"

"Yeah?" He lifted one brow in wry amusement. "You'll what?"

"Nothing. I thought you loved me."

"You know I do."

"Then why are you leaving?"

"You know why? I'm nobody."

"I intend to change that, if you'll let me."

"Yeah? How?"

"I'm going to grant you knighthood and a large parcel of land in the North Country."

"Me? A knight?" He shook his head, amused and amazed by her tenacity. "And then what?"

"And then," she said, her eyes shining with merriment, "we're going to get married again, in front of my family. And I'm going to wear the most beautiful gown you've ever seen. And a long white veil. And a crown."

He couldn't help it. He laughed. And then he drew her into his arms and brushed a kiss across her lips. "Marri, my queen," he said fervently, "I am yours to command, now and for always."

CHAPTER 31

Marri gazed at her reflection in the looking glass, one hand pressed to her abdomen as a million butterflies took flight. Today was her wedding day. Except for the immediate family, no one knew she and Gryff were already married. With that in mind, she knew she should have waited the proper interval after the funerals of her father and brother before marrying Gryff, but she didn't care what people thought. She had waited three months. Three months of pretending he wasn't her husband. Three months of him sneaking into her room after everyone else had retired for the night. She simply couldn't wait another day for everyone to know they were man and wife.

Gryff had been knighted. He now owned several thousand acres in the North Country, as well as his family home in Nardinnia.

"Are you ready, daughter?"

Marri nodded as her mother stepped into the room. Soon all the world would know he belonged to her.

Nardik led Marri to the church located behind the castle. It was a beautiful old building, with stained glass windows and a bell tower. Once she was wed, the bells would ring out the good news.

Marri had asked Nardik to walk her down the aisle and he had graciously accepted. She was surprised at how easily he had slipped into life at the castle, almost as if he had never left.

Though it was customary for all the citizens of Brynn Tor to attend royal weddings if they wished to do so, her mother had decided that, with the recent deaths of the king and his son, it wouldn't be seemly. Therefore, only the king's widow, esteemed members of the clergy, and the rulers of the prominent city-states would be allowed to attend.

Now, walking down the aisle toward the altar, Marri was oblivious to everyone in attendance save for the tall, dark-haired man standing beside the priest. Save that he was clad in white instead of black, Gryff looked much as he had the first time she had seen him—dark and handsome and dangerous. Little had she known then how closely their lives would entwine, or that he would become the most important person in her life.

She smiled at Nardik as he placed her hand in Gryff's.

Obviously feeling ill-at-ease in the midst of Brynn Tor's ruling class, Gryff managed a smile. Leaning forward, he whispered, "I love you, Marri Donovan."

His gaze locked with hers as they repeated the vows that joined them together as husband and wife in front of Brynn Tor's invited guests.

"You may kiss the bride."

Gryff's smile widened as he drew his wife gently into his arms, lifted her veil, and kissed her in full view of her subjects for the first time.

Again, due to recent events, Amerris suggested they postpone the customary lavish reception following the ceremony, and Marri agreed. There were some who were unhappy with this decision, but Marri felt that, under the circumstances, it was the right thing to do.

Alone in their chambers, Gryff closed and locked the door, then drew his bride into his embrace. Clad in a long white gown, her golden hair spilling over her shoulders, she had never looked more beautiful, more desirable. "I will love you as long as I live."

"And I, you."

"Are you sure this is going to work? Not you and me, but me being your…what am I, exactly? The royal consort?"

"No, silly. You're the king of my heart."

With a shake of his head, he removed her veil, showered her with kisses as he unfastened her dress and lifted it over her head, leaving her clad in only her undergarments and shoes.

He whistled softly, smiled as she blushed from head to foot.

Arching one brow, she undressed him down to his briefs. "That's better."

"Much."

He toed off his boots.

She slipped off her shoes.

He stepped out of his shorts.

She shimmied out of her underwear.

"Like what you see?" she asked.

He waggled his brows at her. "I always have."

She laughed softly as she glanced at his arousal, let out a shriek of anticipation when he

swept her into his arms and carried her to bed.

"Was it so bad?" she asked, a twinkle in her eyes. "Marrying me again?"

He shook his head, then kissed the tip of her nose. "Marri, my sweet, I'll marry you as many times as you wish, because there's no place I'd rather be than here, with you in my arms."

She sighed as he rose over her.

There were no assassins hunting for her.

No vindictive witch searching for him.

They had time now, she thought. All the time in the world.

Epilogue

Gryff stood in the doorway of the Great Hall, his heart swelling with love as he watched Marri instruct their five-year-old son in the art of being a king.

If anyone had told him he would one day be living in Brynn Castle, married to the queen, he would never have believed it. His Marri, Queen of Brynn Tor. She had taken him into her heart, given him a home and a life he had never dreamed of.

Feeling his gaze, she looked up, one hand resting on her swollen belly, a smile lighting her face when she saw him.

Crossing the floor, he pulled her into his arms, felt the baby's lusty kick. Their second child would be born before the end of the year. Marri had assured him this one would be a girl.

Gryff kissed her lightly, ruffled his son's hair. "How's the future king doing?"

Marri smiled at their son. "He's going to be a great ruler."

"Just like his mother."

She looked up at him, her gaze caressing his face. "No regrets, my lord husband?"

"No, love, not one. You've given me everything I ever wanted." He laughed softly when he felt the baby kick again. "And so very much more."

About the Author

Amanda Ashley is one of those rare birds—a California native. She's lived in Southern California her whole life and loves it. She married her high school sweetheart, and they have three sons, all handsome enough to be cover models!

Amanda never intended to be a published author. It just happened. She has always loved to read, though—Mary Stewart, Louis L'Amour, Zane Gray. And then she discovered romance novels. One night, when her husband was at work, and her kids were in bed, and there was nothing on TV, she sat down and started writing a book of her own. And she's been writing ever since.

Amanda also writes historical romances as Madeline Baker. She has published over 90 books and novellas, many of which have appeared on various bestseller lists, including the New York Times and USA Today.

www.amandaashley.net
www.madelinebaker.net

www.ingramcontent.com/pod-product-compliance
Lightning Source LLC
Chambersburg PA
CBHW071527120726
47907CB00013B/1244